John FD Northover was born in Belfast into a forward- and free-thinking Anglo-Irish family who championed equality and the arts. As an award-winning director, he has worked throughout Europe and America but knows that home will always be Holywood.

To the people who made and inspired me, my darling parents, Joe and Stella Northover, I dedicate this, my first book, hoping that it captures their sense of adventure, fun, bloody-mindedness and love of the people and places of Ireland.

John FD Northover

A RIBBON BINDS THEM

AUSTIN MACAULEY PUBLISHERS™

LONDON · CAMBRIDGE · NEW YORK · SHARJAH

A CIP catalogue record for this title is available from the British Library.

ISBN 9781528917438 (Paperback)
ISBN 9781528917445 (Hardback)
ISBN 9781528961899 (ePub e-book)

www.austinmacauley.com

First Published (2019)
Austin Macauley Publishers Ltd
25 Canada Square
Canary Wharf
London
E14 5LQ

Chapter One

Since that very first day at St Brigid's Primary School, they had been friends. Together they had shared a Christmas box of Maltesers, Peter Johnson's acne and what little they had gleaned from an all-too-basic sex education class. Yet nothing could have prepared them for their separate lives. It was as if God was determined to keep them apart. Both Oonagh and Marie had made a pact – they were friends for life and if that meant death and damnation so be it.

Oonagh was always the quiet one. Since peeing herself at the age of five, during Miss Fry's roll call, she was worried about what others would say. Sure, she'd known what to say when her name was called out but the pressure of being so low down the alphabet got to her. Why the hell had she been called O'Callaghan? Tommy Bishop would never have this problem. Besides, boys could hold their wee for ages and 'pee on command' – according to Marie. The humiliation of having to wear pants from Miss Fry's 'special drawer' made Oonagh ashamed. She struggled to lose this shame through application but the worry she could never banish and so, despite her best efforts, at the age of sixteen, she was a hairdressing junior in a wee salon off the Shore Road.

Marie could pee like a boy and although her surname was Downey she felt sorry for her best friend. She'd offered her knickers as comfort in the playground but Oonagh had declined, resigning herself to the itching hardship of line-dried drawers. The thought, like Marie herself, was spontaneous and considerate and the male attention roused by its utterance was an education in itself. Marie, where men were concerned, would always have a backup plan. Oonagh would soldier on in misery.

Together they'd joined Miss Slevin's choir. Yes, they could sing but Oonagh only really wanted a new frock for the Easter concert. Her parents were frugal. Her Da had a job in a Belfast bookies, her Ma cleaned big houses in Stranmillis. Both knew that with a change of wind their Protestant employers would return to their own and the 'bureau' would be their only salvation.

Marie's folks were less cautious. Her mother, who loved the amateur dramatics, always made sure her daughter was a picture. She sewed day and night to provide the latest styles and was always too exhausted when James, her husband, returned from his sales trips. So, Marie was an only child and a Ford Escort James Downey's sole passion.

Annie Slevin's choir was legend. Rehearsals were every lunchtime and after school on Tuesdays and Thursdays – miss one session without a note from home and you were out. For this reason Annie kept a waiting list on her classroom wall – a stark reminder that there was always someone else eager to take your place. P5 was the springboard to stardom. Three years of glory awaited if you made it through the public audition process.

The first week of Mr Teakle's class – in she came. Annie Slevin – the proud owner of an Antrim Road house (left to her by her parents) and a heaving bosom straining under blue floral print. Sean Teakle was thrilled to see her. It was his second year at St Brigid's and this year would be it – this year, he would ask Annie Slevin to the Dance near the Co-op. He blushed when she arrived in his classroom and, standing to greet her, was glad of a pleated pant and a longer jacket.

"Be seated boys and girls, it's time."

With these words the talent scout took control. One by one the children sang their chosen songs. That was the joy of Miss Slevin's selection process; you could sing something you really liked. For weeks, hairbrushes in hand, this class of hopefuls had practised before the wardrobe mirrors in their parents' rooms – hoping that their chart-topper would win her heart. Unlike roll call, this was not an alphabetical process and Marie and Oonagh went one after the other. Oonagh had learned from past experiences and had put a spare pair of knickers in her schoolbag, just in case. Marie had packed spare pants and an extra apple.

Sean Teakle announced the children and their song title. It was his only way of impressing Annie Slevin; after all he hadn't got a car and still lived with his parents on the Ormeau Road.

"Marie Attracta Downey – The Hucklebuck."

In a pink gingham empire-line dress, trimmed with a velvet bow, Marie gave it her all. She didn't know if Miss Slevin liked dancing but the song, once in her, forced Marie to move. Boys bounced along to the chorus and even Sean Teakle saw himself 'twisting his baby in' before long. Marie had learned the song on her week's holiday in Newcastle. It was a great hit with The Pierrots who performed twice a day along the Strand. She and her mother had gone every day and had refined her technique in a caravan under the Mournes. It appeared to be paying off – even 'icy Slevin' seemed to thaw.

"Oonagh Theresa O'Callaghan – Nobody's Child."

Eoin Rafferty giggled as the title was read out. *Bastard Eoin Rafferty,* thought Oonagh as she stood beside Mr Teakle's desk.

"Right Oonagh, begin."

Taking a deep breath, as much to steady herself as to fulfil the song's requirements Oonagh began to sing. She had learned the song in the front room from a gramophone record bought by her father. The tale of the blind neglected orphan had touched her – it made her sad and alive. Oonagh O'Callaghan had felt just like this 'wee boy' until Marie came along. For her, there were 'no mummy's kisses, or no daddy's smiles' – she was not an orphan, but she might as well have been for it was not only with money that her parents seemed frugal.

Sung out, Oonagh returned to her seat and Marie handed her a Granny Smith apple – "Well done, we're in." Oonagh wasn't that confident and worried all weekend. At assembly on Monday morning she waited for her name to be read out. She'd peed before filing in and had put on two pairs of pants as a precaution.

"And now, before you go to class, congratulations to the new batch of St Brigid's singers." Oonagh clapped loudest when Marie's name was read out. Marie whooped when the O'Callaghan family became a singer. It was the only celebration – and short-lived. Oonagh's mother started worrying about the Easter outfit that very afternoon.

The eleven plus put paid to Oonagh's public singing. It had been a difficult year for the O'Callaghans. The cleaning jobs in the big houses had diminished as, one by one; their owners saw a civil rights threat to unionism and thought it best to employ someone 'closer to home'. That's what they told themselves.

9

Oonagh's mother was simply told they just had to let her go and with each guilt-ridden, gifted, royal Doulton rosebud vase she saw her daughter's future diminish; her wings of hope clipped by a 'terrible beauty'. There was no money for Oonagh's extra tuition and she struggled with the puzzles that no one in her household could understand. Her father's desperate comprehension attempts only made things worse and Oonagh knew, at the age of ten and a half, that she would never become a teacher.

Marie had no time for such negativity. Her tutor, paid for by her father's longer absences, would guarantee success. With that in mind, every Wednesday after school, Marie trudged to the Lisburn road. In a house, always cabbage-pungent, Marie allowed coercion. Well fingered language tests with greasy green covers and oily past papers were piled in front of her while Mr Cooper, hand resting on her knee, encouraged speed and logic. She wasn't that fond of Mr Cooper; he sweated a lot and breathed over her like an old Labrador, but Marie was determined to get through and tolerated such indecencies to gain success. Besides, she needed to borrow some books to help her friend whose parents couldn't stretch to after-school fees. Oonagh tried and tried to learn from Marie but she could never tick all the boxes. Eventually, Marie decided it was best if Oonagh studied the books on her own. That way, the girls could laugh again, together.

Apart from Oonagh, no one knew that Marie was taking a bus across town to be tutored by a Protestant. Her lessons, like Mr Cooper's behaviour, were to remain a secret. He wrote reports of promise to the family, tracing his ink-stained fingers along the hem of Marie's frock. He scolded her loudly when she made a mistake but comforted her on his knee when she cried. Many times she was sure she was right only to find his lumpen cavalry twill pressing against her thigh. She knew something was wrong but she needed to better herself and so accepted such personal punishment. It was her secret; the price you paid for not being in the Orange Order.

The final term at St Brigid's before the 'big exam' was Miss Slevin's last so the concert that Easter was extra special. No one really knew why Annie Slevin was leaving. There had been talk. Talk in the staff room and in the playground. Mrs Lavery, the

Head, was annoyed by her resignation. Women teachers who didn't want babies were hard to come by; single women with no maternal instincts – a rarity. Devotion was going out of fashion so why had Annie Slevin tried to ruin the family that was St Brigid's. "Well Annie, I'm shocked and disappointed – is there nothing we can do to persuade you to stay?"

"It's not been an easy decision…but it is time to move on."

"But where will you go? What will you do?"

"I don't quite know as yet – a bit of travel – maybe an adventure. I need to set aside the little girl from the Antrim road and free the woman within me."

"Oh I see." Clearly, Mrs Lavery didn't. Women's libbers were alien to her. Was Annie Slevin one of those lesbians after all? Was she a lover of Sylvia Plath? Perhaps the occasional dates with Sean Teakle had driven her to it. He was too, too soft. Deirdre Lavery stood and hugged her colleague. Annie felt as if she had already left. The last time Deirdre Lavery had shown such restrained affection was outside St Colmcilles' when Annie had buried her father. "Well," mumbled Deirdre, recovering from such an emotional outburst, "Let's give them a concert to remember."

"But of course," smiled Annie, "and thank you." With that Annie Slevin returned to break duty, back to the children to whom, once, she had belonged.

Sean Teakle blamed himself. They'd only been stepping out since Christmas and already Annie was planning to abandon him. The staff room was unbearable. Evil looks from kind colleagues were the worst. Had he made her pregnant? Perhaps she wants marriage and he doesn't? Perhaps there is something we don't know about that Sean Teakle: what has he done to make our Annie want to leave? The tongues wagged and Annie couldn't silence them. Sean Teakle didn't figure in her plans. Her decision had nothing to do with him.

"Teakle's got her up the duff," announced Danny Burn.

"What?"

"Teakle's made a baby with Miss Slevin. She doesn't want it and that's why she's leaving."

Oonagh and Marie watched and watched but there was no sign of a baby. Danny Burn was always first with the news and always wrong in the end; a tabloid journalist in the making. Still the story grew and grew and St Brigid's Easter concert was a sell-out.

That year as every Easter, Paddy cursed as he brushed. Pink cherry blossom was the cause. A solitary tree in the corner of the school grounds annually challenged him with an endless supply of petals. Paddy liked order – what point being a caretaker if no care is taken? – and so for two hours before the concert he brushed and cursed. The boss, Mrs Lavery, had done her best with the lunchtime litter hunt but children have no love of neatness and Paddy wouldn't let St Brigid's down. She alone had kept him on the straight and narrow: a single pioneer in a world of chaotic coupledom. He should love the tree for her but Paddy Tully's world had no room for feminine touches, perhaps he should have been born a Protestant after all.

Alone on the Antrim Road Annie Slevin had soaked in lavender, applied rose water and glycerine and was now tending to her hair. She'd be sorry to leave the children, but each brush stroke made her long for freedom. Change was in the air and, with her parents dead, she had no ties. Before rebellion she would sell up and follow her heart. Italy, the home of song, was her secret passion and her pink Avon lipstick would see her through the lonely times.

In separate houses Oonagh and Marie scrubbed in parallel. They had been let off school early to prepare. A bonus for them, this caused confusion in their households. Marie was surprised to find an orange Skoda in her street. Very few of the neighbours had cars and no one she knew owned such a triumphalist vehicle. She let herself in, as she always did, and was shocked to find Mr Cooper in the front room. He smelled of Brut and rubbed his damp palms down his trousers before shaking her hand. "Mr Cooper is going to drive us to the concert in his new car," said her mother slightly flustered, "Won't that be nice?" Marie nodded and went upstairs with her things. Ashamed of her mother, ashamed of Mr Cooper's hideous Protestant car, ashamed of herself, she scrubbed the flannel dry and her skin pure. A new dress of pale green lay on the bed. Her mother had taken weeks to make it, spending hours in Robb's choosing the fine lace to trim the sleeves. If only she hadn't trimmed the hem Marie might have been able to wear the dress on weekdays. Still, it suited her colouring and as she put it on Marie vowed to sing better than anyone, ever.

Oonagh O'Callaghan had no new outfit. Times were hard in the O'Callaghan household. The bookies, where her dad had worked, had been petrol bombed and showed no sign of ever opening again. The Grosvenor Road had changed so Oonagh's dad was helping wire houses in East Belfast. Someone somewhere had money but it wasn't in Oonagh's part of town. Oonagh would wear last year's dress, the hem let down and hand sewn, but by way of understanding Maeve O'Callaghan plaited new ribbons in her daughter's hair. Each twist of pale green satin increased understanding and love: although unfortunate the O'Callaghans' were lucky in their misfortune.

Sean Teakle had a new shirt and tie. He had bought it on Saturday before the GAA match. It was a set so you didn't need to put the two things together yourself – some bloke in Dublin had chosen for you. The gent's outfitters near the Spinning Mill was the perfect choice of shop – he was a teacher after all. He couldn't cope with Anderson and McAuley. The fey shop assistants in there always looked down on him, or so it seemed, and even when they called him 'sir' he felt inadequate. No, 'Corr and Sons' would do for him. Besides, they were a lot cheaper and although he wished to impress Annie Slevin it would not be a sound investment as she had already decided to leave. The collar, in fact the whole shirt, was stiff and made him ill at ease. Against his mother's advice, and to assert his masculinity, he had abandoned his vest and the cold coarse cotton felt odd against his skin. His neck would be red raw before the day was out but, what the hell! – he was damned if he would look abandoned for anyone and after all no one would see him at the close of day. If casting a clout before May was out resulted in pneumonia, it would be better than the shame of looking hen-pecked and forlorn that evening.

Pale blue Crimplene was Mrs Lavery's choice for the concert. She'd bought the two-piece for her niece's wedding but on learning that a Presbyterian Church was the venue she had never seen fit to wear it. The wedding had been a small affair. Her sister had understood and had gone along for her daughter's sake but the St Brigid's principle, head of school, community and family, could not be seen to condone such treachery. She'd sent a gift of Waterford crystal to remind her niece of her heritage. A thank you card was their only communication after that. To complement the outfit cream shoes were unboxed, a cream bag unwrapped. No singing teacher, resigning or otherwise, would take Deirdre Lavery's crown.

The concert was to start at half past six, just after tea, but all were too excited to eat. Besides, there would be buns and sandwiches from the Parish ladies after the singing and the nuns had lent a couple of urns for the tea.

Nerves and cold leather made Marie's dress cling to her thighs. The car journey was awful. Marie felt no pride as Mrs Downey giggled and Mr Cooper frequently apologised for touching her knee as he changed gear. They thought Marie didn't notice but nothing escaped her. *Get through the eleven plus, then we shall both be rid of him,* she thought. It was a relief when they parked on the road just down from the school gates. Marie jumped out and ran to greet Oonagh – partly to disassociate herself from her mother's ecumenical antics but mainly to escape the bulbous hands of a private tutor. "We're wearing the same colour."

"Well, sort of," smiled Oonagh. "How great – those ribbons are fab." Marie knew all the right words and when to use them, thought Oonagh. No wonder she had a solo this evening. No wonder they were friends.

In a hall full of age and no age, chalk dust and weakened bleach, Father Fullerton rose to his feet. As priest of the parish it was fitting that he should give the welcome speech but just how fitting only Annie Slevin knew. They'd been Antrim Road neighbours for years before his calling. Morning and evening they had shared tea and toast, a love of music and a passion for learning so it was strange, wild strange that their religion should have divided them. As teenagers they had taken trains to Bangor, walked in Helen's Bay, and kissed at Castlewellan but Declan was an only son and his devout parents longed for a priest in the family. Maynooth at seventeen for him, St Mary's for her. They'd written but the letters, like his religion, were exacting and she felt unable to freely express her love. Her parents never asked after Declan – they didn't wish to encourage unreality. It was after her father's funeral that tea and toast again became a habit – a symbol of their past, a comfort in times of need.

He had been shocked to learn of her plans; finally he would be near her and she was leaving. Naivety was always Declan's problem. His new proximity was unbearable for her. He was married to his God and the pain of longing was more than she could bear. She had not the level of sin within to force his hand; to leave the priesthood would be to murder his mother without bloodshed. How could she ask him to do so? The escape from Ireland was her solution.

As Declan welcomed his parish she knew this was where he belonged. His gentle qualities of leadership were obvious to all. She watched her choir gaze at him in awe and as he spoke with affection of her attributes the fragrance of lavender and rose intensified. She bowed her head as applause rang out and asked her God for the strength to continue. She smiled a smile that only secret lovers know and he bowed his head in acknowledgement. Walking centre stage she shook his hand, he double clasped hers and took his seat on the platform between Sister Francois and Mrs Lavery. One by one the children filed onto the stage and nailed their feet to the wooden tiers. An artistic arrangement borne of practicality, it guaranteed that every proud parent could see the object of their pride and that the St Vincent de Paul coffers were filled once again.

Annie Slevin had chosen well, for she had chosen from the heart, and this year's choir sounded better than she could have hoped. The singers knew of her departure and wished pure sounds and clean harmonies to be their farewell gift. Sure, there was a summer term but there'd be no more Slevin recitals. Marie and Oonagh felt it most, even more perhaps than Father Fullerton and so they sang with a surety beyond their years.

'Sally Gardens' for her mother; 'Mountains of Mourne' for her father; 'Ave Marie' for Marie Downey and 'The Carnival is over' for Declan and herself. As her close classes sang close harmony, Annie Slevin embraced the Seekers' lyrics with her very soul hoping that Declan would hear their true significance. She did not need to hope – he was all too aware that this break in tradition was for him and him alone. He wanted to pick her up there and then and run for freedom but shackled between religion and education, as he was now and always seemed to be, flight was impossible.

Oonagh cried twice during the concert. Not for Marie Downey and her solo, not for Annie Slevin and her empty carnival but for herself. She knew this was her finest hour. She knew that a life of disappointment was hers for the taking, but she also knew that pale green ribbons would bind her with Marie forever.

The after concert tea was grand. Mrs Liddy and her team made sure of that. School lunches were one thing but here they had a chance to shine. Chocolate mice, rice krispie buns, marshmallow top hats and fifteens appeared by the tray load. As the grownups ate triangles of ham and salad, the choir gorged on sugar fancies, too innocent for adulthood. The caramel squares were Oonagh's favourites so she wrapped some in a napkin for later, one for her and one for Eoin Rafferty – if she could find him! Marie kept lookout by the fifteens as Oonagh snatched her prize. Mrs Downey had taken to making tins of tray bakes just in case she had visitors and caramel squares were Mr Cooper's favourites. Marie had had her fill of those and her dad didn't even like sweet things. How she longed to be like Miss Slevin, untamed by boys, in perfumed control and off on a new adventure. "Marie Downey, you've a grand voice, your parents must be very proud."

"I think so, Father – Mum's here with Mr Cooper and Dad's in Galway."

"Still I'm sure he will hear about it soon – I'll be sure to tell him if no one else does." Father Fullerton patted Marie on the head and thought better of having a word with Mrs Downey. He didn't trust the Cooper one but couldn't work out why. It wasn't the flash car or the beige pants, nor was it his sniffing round another man's wife. It was something sinister that, like the existence of God, he only knew but couldn't prove. "Leave some of those fifteens for the children." Declan Fullerton laughed at Annie's reprimand, the first laugh they had shared in ages. "Besides I have a cake to cut and I'll need your help with that." Mrs Liddy had made a cake sure enough. "Congratulations – Miss Slevin and the Choir of 69." The message, like the cake was plain enough – iced sponge, like the birthday cakes bought on the Stranmillis Road – plain but posh. A protestant-looking cake in a wee Catholic School; yet, cakes have no religion and so it was greeted warmly by all when trolleyed in. Oonagh

16

O'Callaghan missed her piece. She was sharing a caramel square with Eoin Rafferty by the caretaker's lockup. Eoin gave her tuppence to put his hand in her knickers. It was the easiest money Oonagh ever earned.

Chapter Two

The Eleven Plus was a disaster for both girls for the results were predictable. Marie, with her Protestant tutor and inbred desire for achievement, passed perfectly; while Oonagh, who so needed the opportunity, was branded a failure. Marie's new bike helped her cycle to her friend's house but for Oonagh its shiny new paintwork and silver bell constantly increased her sense of inadequacy. Moneyed parents offered pass incentives to their children; Oonagh had merely been encouraged to 'do her best'. She had tried with all her heart. At Mass she'd secretly prayed to God for a miracle, she'd asked the Blessed Virgin to guide her. In the evenings, when she should have been staring from the front room window she was locked in her bedroom trying to make sense of Marie's borrowed books; if only she could have borrowed Marie's head, that might just have made a difference. As it was the more she prayed for clarity the more confused she became. Her mother worried. Her father sighed. Neither had had much of an education; no convent or Christian Brother had welcomed them. They'd both left school early to embrace disappointment and accept realistic expectations. Still, they wanted more for Oonagh. Life was hard and an education was something to fall back on. With that you could get an office job in town and a hire purchase agreement at the Co-Op. Once the O'Callaghans had tried for a new three-piece suit on 'easy-terms' but the paperwork and their address had defeated them. With an education Oonagh might one day have a dining table. Their vain hopes dashed again, they hugged their daughter as she cried with disappointment. Looking at each other, they saw her future in their own and vowed to pretend it wouldn't matter.

As James and Moira Downey proudly unveiled the new red bike Marie concealed her disappointment. Yes, the bike was lovely, but in a house two streets away her best friend had failed again and that made her passing worse. "Isn't it great James, our daughter a grammar school girl?"

"A Convent girl, no less," smiled Mr Downey, picking up his car keys and heading for the door. Strange that a convent was their choice. For years Marie had been threatened with the nuns at Kilkeel if she misbehaved and in September, a version of that threat could be a reality. Sister Ignatius at the Sacred Heart hadn't been all that frightening when they were interviewed after Easter – perhaps Nuns were always pleasant after the Resurrection. Besides, Dunmurry was miles from Kilkeel and although the Order was the same Marie decided that only evil Nuns, the man-hating, child-hating Sisters of God were kept in that fishing village Nunnery. Rathmore might be all right but the burgundy uniform would never get her noticed. "A caramel square with your tea?" A calloused hand lifted the homemade offering onto a china plate.

"Well done Marie," chomped Mr Cooper. "University next – Queen's of course, that's where we'll aim."

The ghastly orange car was nowhere to be seen – well that was small comfort for Marie and also strangely for Thomas Cooper. This area was not what it was. Flags had been appearing; the wrong sort of flags, and Thomas Cooper couldn't risk car loss. A burnt out orange Skoda was no use to him in the summer. He'd walked from the Lisburn Road and was still sweating as he drank his tea. "So, I suppose you are off to celebrate now that you have your new bike?" Marie just looked at him. "Marie, Mr Cooper's speaking to you. After all it's mainly thanks to him that you are off to Rathmore."

Bollocks, thought Marie. *It's thanks to me and my keeping my mouth shut.*

"Marie?" Moira Downey looked sternly at her daughter and sharply replaced her teacup in its saucer. "I'll ride over to Oonagh's and…" Marie didn't feel at all like celebrations. "…Thank you for teaching me and eh… for the pencil set."

"My pleasure," dripped Mr Cooper. "Can I go now?"

"Yes, but be careful and be back by 4 pm. I've got to go to Andersonstown for some messages and tell Oonagh we are sorry for her." Marie closed the front door behind her and wheeled her bike down the passage. She hid her red trophy round the back of the house and walked the two streets to Oonagh's.

It was the first of many such trips. Marie was often round at Oonagh's that summer, especially when James Downey was home. All her parents did was argue. Marie didn't know what it was all about. The Downeys unlike the O'Callaghans had money but both sets of parents seemed equally miserable. Marie scrutinised Oonagh's parents. They were nothing like her own. James Downey was always touching Moira when she was at the sink when she did the dishes, as she hovered the front room, as she changed the beds but his hands were always quickly removed, brushed off with a 'not now James' or a 'can't you see I'm busy'. The O'Callaghans never got on like that. They just looked at each other. *Perhaps for them,* thought Marie, *that is enough.* They, having nothing to give, gave nothing. At least they were consistent; they'd always been like that. Marie's parents, like Belfast, were changing and she didn't like it. There was tension in the household when her Dad was home. Times that should have been happy were spoilt by unanticipated disagreements. Mealtimes were the worst. The littlest thing could set them off; a goulash too foreign, a gammon too salty, no pudding just 'bloody wee buns'. Something wasn't quite right and Marie was sure it was all her fault. She was dumbfounded when, just after the twelfth fortnight, a time of limited movement and little pleasure, her parents proposed a week in Newcastle. They'd even offered to take Oonagh with them and, after several failed attempts at persuasion, the O'Callaghans reluctantly agreed that it would be 'good for her'.

Chapter Three

Newcastle was special for the Downeys, that's why James had suggested it. His wife had taken some persuading but just like at bedtime, he always got his way in the end. James Downey could be quite forceful when needed.

The town itself was little more than a main street but at one end stretched magical mountains and at right angles a glorious beach. Moira and James had come here when first married. They'd stayed with Kitty Tier in her grey stoned guesthouse near the saltwater baths. She was a forthright no nonsense woman who cooked a mean breakfast. Half board was where she excelled – who could go wrong with a ham salad, and with a tomato-growing husband and an endless production line of homemade wheaten her profit margins were sound. This, and a brother an accountant, kept her in business. She was only too pleased to book the big room at the front for the Downeys and to put in an extra bed for 'the other wee girl'. James would have preferred an extra room but in high season 'beggars can't be choosers' and Mrs Tier only had one cancellation. How it had annoyed her. The Billingtons had been coming for the last ten years; A lovely couple from Kent. He worked on the aircraft and she was a civil servant but recent news reports had troubled them and, despite Mrs Tier's reassurances and their loss of deposit, the holiday friendship ceased. Kitty Tier had wished them well and told them to keep in touch. She feared they wouldn't. They never did.

The O'Callaghans handed Oonagh over at ten o'clock as arranged. They had made a special effort for they knew how judgemental Moira Downey was. Oonagh's Dad had cleared out a small suitcase from under the wardrobe. He'd given it a wash and sprayed it with too much of his wife's dressing table perfume. For years it had held his boyhood secrets but, for the sake of his daughter, he'd let those go in a bin in the yard. It was bad enough that Oonagh had failed her exam; he couldn't let her travel with a paper carrier bag. "She looks like a refugee – poor little thing." James Downey ignored his wife's pity. It was typical of her not to notice the holiday ribbons so carefully plaited in Oonagh's hair. "Well," said Mr O'Callaghan, "she's all yours."

"We'll look after her Padraig, don't worry."

"She's got some spending money," piped up Maeve O'Callaghan, "and there's a wee note of Mrs O'Connor's number if you need to contact us." *How sad that they don't have a telephone of their own,* thought Moira. "Don't worry, she'll be fine – right girls in you get."

Oonagh took some persuading to let go of her new case but after Marie assured her that nothing could happen to it in the boot the girls clambered onto the back seat. They waved frantically as the car drove away. The O'Callaghan's waved back and Oonagh thought they looked sad. Would they be all right with no one to look after them? That consideration added to her already present worries. She'd packed all the summer clothes she needed for a week by the sea. She'd packed all the summer clothes she had. Fortunately she had a new swimming costume; a grown up all in one in ruched navy and white. It was her mother's final addition to the holiday packing, after the 'just in case holiday pants' and the 'you never know cardigan'. Maeve O'Callaghan was thrilled with her last minute purchase. It was the only one on the end of season discount rail and she knew as she held it up in the shop that it would fit Oonagh perfectly. She couldn't stretch to the navy Scholl flip-flops that would have matched it so last year's summer sandals would just have to do. Beside Oonagh's tan vinyl case, nestling between a cream vanity case and a masculine holdall was Marie Downey's summer wardrobe – a sweatshop of new outfits for the holiday. It was a convent girl's summer wardrobe – handpicked, handmade and perfectly complimenting the outfits of an irreverent mother. Oonagh had no idea of what daily delights were in store but Marie had removed the white Scholl flip-flops "to keep them for best." With the time for leaving growing ever closer, Moira Downey had given in. Mr Cooper was right. Marie's independent streak needed to be watched.

The girls were beside each other with excitement. Oonagh had never been away from home let alone stayed in a guesthouse. Marie had caravanned in Newcastle and knew the town but she'd only ever had her mother for company and had never stayed at 'Tall Trees', the guesthouse where she was made. Her dad had pointed it out once on the way to the caravan site, causing her mother to giggle and to tap him on the shoulder, but this time Marie would actually be going in, saying hello to Mrs Tier, and hopefully, rediscovering her parents' joy.

Everything was new to Oonagh: a gable wall remembering 1690, red, white and blue paving stones, a red hand of Ulster. As they crossed town she absorbed their strangeness. No one else seemed bothered. Mrs Downey folded and refolded a road map, Mr Downey kept his eye on the road and Marie struggled with a family bag of Raspberry Ruffles. It was then that Oonagh remembered her stamps. She checked that all three were still in her purse. Da had given them to her to keep safe until she found postcards. Three stamps for the four most important people in her life – Nana Downey, Granny Tulley and her parents. The fifth most important person now offered her a raspberry ruffle. Oonagh declined for fear her stamps would stick together. Marie nodded and placed two sweets between them before handing the split bag to her mother. Soon, without the use or acknowledgement of his wife's navigational skills, James Downey guided them to the open road.

An hour into the journey, and not before time, Mr Downey pulled the Ford Escort into the side of the road. While the girls clambered over a fence to create an outside toilet he erected a newly acquired windbreak and got the primus stove to light – after the fourth attempt. Moira unfolded the two deckchairs, the girls would have to make do with the car rug, and set out the Tupperware sandwiches. She'd learnt all this from Thomas Cooper while James was away and it comforted her to know that Thomas was also here in the practicalities. "Isn't this great?" said James deftly removing grass from his egg and onion sandwich. No one replied. The sunshine drying Oonagh's wee-dampened sock was a worry to Mrs Downey and so no sooner had they began their picnic than they were back in the car feeling hot, "stomachy" and wondering just how long this trip would take. Every time Mr Downey said 'not long now', the journey seemed to take longer. Two water refills, a stop for a cool down, one wrong turning and a chemist hunt all took their toll and lunch was well over when they arrived at 'Tall Trees'. Marie thought it an odd name for a treeless house and decided to share her concern with Mrs Tier on better acquaintance.

"Twelve years – is it really?" smiled Mrs Tier showing the quartet to their room. "The bathroom is just next door and the evening meal is at 6pm as usual. If you ever want to eat out just tell me the day before and I'll give you a packed lunch instead at no extra charge."

"That's very kind, Mrs Tier."

"Now dear, call me Kitty. Sure we are all one big happy family here."

It isn't and we're not, thought James but he smiled to please his wife, or hoped he did. The carefully packed suitcases, unpacked just as carefully by Moira Downey, were put under the bed and the West Belfast holidaymakers set off to take in the sights. James suggested chips and ice cream and the girls suddenly remembered they were starving. They ran ahead down the little hill from Mrs Tier's but a little scared of their new environment, waited on the corner for the parents to catch them up. "I think it's round here to the left," said James, and so it was; an odd restaurant cum shop with a window hatch for ice creams. Oonagh had never seen such a pick 'n' mix. They took a booth for four by the window. The lower half was frosted to protect the diner's dignity and, on either side of the table, Marie and Oonagh watched eerie-bubbled shapes on their way to and from the beach. The seats were covered in the latest dark brown vinyl that, although initially cold, soon became hot and sticky. Salt, pepper, a vinegar bottle and a giant plastic tomato were the only dressing on the melamine table. Soon, however, it was littered with plates of white bread and butter, cups of tea, glasses of Fanta and the best chips the girls had ever tasted. Moira Downey struggled with a cod and chips and in the end James not only ate his but also half of hers. James Downey hated waste. A woman in a pink nylon overall cum housecoat gave them the bill – "Pay at the counter on your way out. Was everything alright?"

"Lovely, thank you," replied a guilty Moira Downey. Did this young madam know she had only eaten half? Marie watched the girl's drop earrings quiver as she turned on her heel to the next table. She longed for pierced ears. She longed to deck herself in hoops and crosses but she knew it wouldn't be this summer. Oonagh didn't notice the waitress' earrings. She was staring at Mr Downey's wallet. He was counting out the money to cover the bill. There was a funny clip thing keeping the notes together – now what was the point of that – wondered Oonagh. As he fingered the pound notes Oonagh thought the Downeys very rich. Not only had they bought Marie a bike but they had a flash car and had taken the biggest room at Tall Trees. James Downey refolded the notes, clipped them together and with an "ice cream, girls?" encouraged departure. They slid towards the chequered aisle and headed to the till. "I'll just go and powder my nose James and don't get any ice cream for me." Moira Downey adjusted her dress and headed towards the ladies.

At the till a freckled girl got confused with someone else's change. The girls weren't worried; it gave them time to choose Oyster, Poke or Slider. Marie chose a slider, bright white ice cream, two wafers and some blood red sauce. It came in a square of waxed paper and started to drip on handover, "What will it be, Oonagh?" Although the Oyster looked and sounded more exotic Oonagh copied her friend. Mr Downey also had a Slider but his had a special chocolate nougat addition that was too grown up for either girl. "Lovely facilities," announced Moira Downey as they left Caproni's. The girl at the till smiled, acknowledged the praise and instantly branded Moira a stuck up townie.

Marie and Oonagh giggled and licked wrist, hand and ice cream in a futile attempt to keep the red and white liquids at bay. They placed the remains, two squares of waxed paper, in a wasp-attracting bin and borrowed a handkerchief to wipe their sticky fingers. Returning the sugar-coated kerchief to her handbag, Moira commanded all to stop at Newcastle's finest gift shop. The double windows were crammed with Newcastle spoons, thimbles, bottle openers and ashtrays. Connemara marble slabs and Belleek butter dishes vied for attention with poetic dishcloths and table bells. Sandwiched between the amusement arcade and the rock shop this was Moira Downey's holiday haven. None of the party ventured in. It was too early to be buying souvenirs so she suggested a dip in the fresh water pool near the guesthouse. Not for her of course. She'd had enough of her husband for one day and so, feigning a headache, she went for a lie down while James crossed the road to the baths.

The girls had put on their costumes under their clothes but James still had to hold their rolled up towels as they pushed their way through the turnstile. He paid, 'two children and one adult,' and went off to find the gentlemen's changing area. Oonagh and Marie waited for him beside the blue and white huts watching as old men swam and young boys bombed in the bright blue water. James Downey, towel under arm was a fine figure of a man. Oonagh tried not to look but the navy belted trunks caught her eye. She'd never seen her Da that naked and wondered if his bulge was as big as Mr Downey's. Marie was too busy finding them somewhere to sit where they wouldn't get wet to notice Oonagh's fascination. "Over here," she bawled, "I'm over here!" Oonagh clambered up the concrete steps to join her. They spread their towels on the woodened covered tierings and arranged their sandals beside the beach bag that contained their clothes. No sooner were all three settled than a swim was called for. To call it swimming is to lie; it was really more of a dip. As they bobbed about in the shallow end they barely noticed the white clouds gather overhead. Greyed by the sight of the approaching Mournes the clouds soon unleashed a fine spray of rain, which briefly warmed the icy water and encouraged the girls to squeal louder. Towards five o'clock the grey clouds blackened and rods of rain pierced the pool.

Wrapped in his damp towel, wet beach bag in hand, James led his two migratory seabirds across the road to their holiday nest. The rain bounced off the pavement and into their wet sandals. They were soaked head to toe and as they dripped up the guesthouse stairs all three began to giggle. Moira Downey, scowling at them from the bedroom door, only made it more laughable. "Welcome to sunny Newcastle," she added as they padded into the room. A wet faced James kissed her on the cheek – the rest must have done her some good surely.

It rained all through tea. Both Oonagh and Marie watched droplets of disappointment bounce off the steely glass in the dining room. As new guests they had the window table. It had been reserved for the Billingtons but on learning of their demise, Mrs Tier had quickly added two extra chairs. Moira Downey was delighted with this arrangement. It was the best table in the room and she was honoured that 'Kitty' had reserved it just for her. The pre-plated salad arrived – eventually. After the late lunch Moira was worried that the girls would pick over it, eating little, but the short pool visit had re-awakened their appetites so her worry was in vain.

Marie liked the orange and purple jellies that melted between cold lettuce and chopped scallions. She explained to Oonagh that this was a very posh person's salad. Oonagh forked the mandarin, carrot and jelly concoction. The carrots, although grated, were still crunchy – she wasn't sure about them at all, but the squelchy tinned mandarins enveloped in sweet jelly appeased her and helped her swallow the hard rectangle of processed ham. She couldn't tackle the circle of stuffed pork luncheon meat. It reminded her of Spam and she hated that. With theatrical aplomb Marie dropped a forkful of beetroot jelly all down her white lace blouse, "Come quickly Marie, we'll have to soak that." Before she could protest Moira Downey ushered Marie out of the Dining Room. The five other guests smiled in confused acknowledgement – too busy marvelling at the thinly sliced eggs that decorated their plates.

In the kitchen Kitty Tier practised with her new gadget. She'd bought the metal and wire contraption at the Ideal Home Exhibition in Blackpool on an Ulster bus coach trip to visit her sister. Unlike the holiday trip, the egg slice was a success. Perfectly matched slices, teased under pressure, were this year's salad addition. An English design it made eggs go further. Kitty couldn't get away with English portions here. Ulster would have most definitely have said no to that but this fine slicing and the addition of coloured jellies might just help Kitty acquire the flock wallpaper for the hall.

Alone with Oonagh, James Downey felt compelled to speak. "So Oonagh, what shall we do after tea?" It was an unfair question, as Oonagh had no idea of her options. "We could go for another swim."

"In this weather, has the change of air made you giddy?"

"No, I err…" Oonagh again felt stupid. She'd never been to the seaside before – that afternoon had been her only holiday experience to date. "I'll tell you what, we'll take a walk into town when the rain clears and make our plans for tomorrow."

The return of mother and daughter was a relief to all. Marie now wore a yellow flowery dress with a belt that tied at the side. Oonagh noted that she'd changed her shoes as well and felt doubly jealous. They finished their salads in silence. All, apart from Marie, cleared their plates. She left a guilty claret-coloured mountain that slowly spread across the white china. A gangly girl cleared the tables in a pre-determined order and Kitty Tier replaced the debris with a pot of tea and some iced buns. They were not from a packet but homemade. Sure they seemed familiar to Oonagh but tasted different. Such sense of difference forced restraint. Oonagh was confused by new things, concerned by change. Marie tucked in, even if it made her sick, she'd give anything a go – unless her appearance could be threatened. This was her last summer of carefree eating. Under her mother's guidance she would become a victim. Constantly on diets – mathematically chewing cubes of fudge-like diet suppressants, pre aids Ayds. Constantly measuring, vomiting, scissor-jumping and skipping to acquire her mother's frame. That evening, three iced buns gave her guilt-free pleasure. "Now, that's enough Marie. Think of the starving children in Africa. James, tell her."

"I don't think the black babies would mind, Moira," then sensing his wife's wind changed face, "but your mother's right, that's quite enough eating for one day. Besides, we've got to plan tomorrow before bedtime. Let's take the girls along the front, Moira."

Like the dog in the back of Fat Coopers car, Moira Downey smiled and nodded her way out of the dining room. The rain had given up and the air was damp with girlish excitement. Two by two, girls in front, parents behind, they headed into town. They stopped on a bridge over the boating lake watching a red-faced youth struggle to extricate a numbered boat from the weir. A red-faced woman giggled assistance to no avail. "Why don't we take a boat out tomorrow?" suggested Moira. The girls' delight forced James to put that into the plan. The red-faced man eventually rolled up his trousers, got into the water and pushed the boat free. Marie and Oonagh were saddened at the lack of depth. If only he'd drowned, now that could have been something to put in the postcard to Granny Tully. She loved to hear of people dying – especially if she knew them. Granny Tully had endless tales of sadness to please her. No one in the death columns escaped her beady eyes. Her satisfaction at recognising a name puzzled Oonagh. Did she hate her friends that much? Aileen Tully dearly loved her friends and family. Death for her was the final answer in a crossword puzzle – a five-letter word that never went across. It always went down into the City Cemetery but there were many ways of getting to it. The red-faced boy and girl reddened further when they saw the crowd on the bridge. They tried to ignore the noise by rowing quickly in the opposite direction, but the lack of skill that had grounded them was still in evidence and their humiliation grew. Two passing swans looked at them with disdain.

Losing interest in this 'common couple', Moira Downey lead the family with its charity addition down the main street, quickly past the amusement arcade which seemed to fascinate both her husband and the children, past O'Donoghue's pub which also seemed an attraction and to the row of shops before the Slieve Donard Hotel. Moira Downey would buy a wee cardigan from the ladies outfitters before their return to Belfast. Their proximity to the grandest hotel in the county made these shops more appealing to the Downeys. To Oonagh all shops appealed for she seldom had any money to permit entry. It was typical now her purse was full the shops were closed. Having arrived at the end of the town they mirrored their steps on the other side of the street. An early night was the reward for such a trek and as they settled in for the evening the rain returned washing away all dreams of sunburn.

The unmistakable smell of Denny's rashers and Cookstown sausages roused them. Even in the summer Ulster fried. Fearful of being late down to breakfast Moira Downey ushered the girls along the corridor to the bathroom, kept watch as they flannelled themselves clean and nipped in when they had finished for her own speedy toilette. Pristine and ravenous the Downey girls sat down to breakfast. James, unapproved by Moira, had decided to shave later. Thomas Cooper would never be seen bearded at breakfast, holiday or not. The cornflakes from the Tupperware jug were surprisingly crisp and helped keep conversation to a minimum. A triumphant Kitty soon arrived at table one with four cooked breakfasts and, "An extra sausage for Mr Downey, why with three women to control, you'll need to keep your strength up." James smiled and thanked Mrs Downey for her concern and generosity. The girls tucked in to the warm delicacies with haste. This was a real holiday breakfast – fried soda and potato bread, bacon, sausage, a fried egg and, as a concession to any English visitor, a piece of grilled tomato. All was washed down with a fresh pot of tea and complimented by white toast and jam.

The after breakfast toilet procession was as regimented as the breakfast itself and, once finished, freed all for a grand day at the seaside. Mrs Tier's packed lunch option in one hand and their beach bags in the other, the occupants of table one set off across the road. With the restlessness of new discovery they climbed a small wall, clambered down the rocks soon landing on the damp sand. Moira Downey would have preferred to take the newly crafted council steps but assured by James that she would be all right, gave in to the girls' carefree ways. Whilst the girls stretched their towels out on the sand, James struggled with undress. Since youth he had struggled. Considerable manual dexterity was required to hold the towel, ease off the jockey pants and snake into the trunks. Often his mother had assisted by holding the towel and looking away when he was a boy but, now a man; there was no such help. He had noticed the O'Callaghan girl's stares yesterday at the pool and this made him more self-conscious today. Why hadn't he put his costume on before breakfast? With a final male adjustment he removed the worn striped beach towel and began to relax. Moira was busy applying baby oil to anyone who stood still long enough and the girls, covered in youthful grease, began the Northern Irish process of skin burn. An unsettled Moira unsettled James and no sooner had he stretched out than he was sitting up again answering her questions. Were they going to visit his old friend Neil McConaghy? Should they take a run out in the car tomorrow? Was Kitty Tier a bit run down? James considered all these possibilities but committed to nothing. He had learnt over the years to let his wife both ask and answer her own questions. It made for happier times at home. He had given up hope of a son through answering too many questions. Marie's birth had been difficult – they'd lost two babies in the run up and the doctor had been all too quick to answer not only Marie's questions but also his. Another child would be too dangerous. God had agreed with the doctor and so despite their many clandestine attempts his seed never took. Moira had thrown herself into her new daughter and St Agnes' Choral Society. She enjoyed the singing and the annual show and was thrilled that she may have passed such enjoyment on to her daughter. James loved his wife but their lack of goal in the bedroom made sex one-sided. For Moira it was all about 'making babies' and now that babies were 'ill advised', she thought they didn't need to try so much. However, since a sales trip to Harrogate with Declan Maguire James Downey discovered other reasons for this activity. That Easter James Downey was bored; bored of Belfast, bored of his wife and frightened that he might be bored of himself. Two days in Harrogate changed all that, for a time.

Declan Maguire was a bit of a lad. Good at his job, good with the ladies. Despite too much Guinness on the boat, the shared drive to Harrogate was uneventful. They stayed in The Old Swan in the centre of town – such luxury had escaped either of them until now and on the second night of their two-day stay they found a little more than their bearings. In a bar off the main road, not far from the Conference Centre, they'd found Sheila and her friend Eileen. These girls were forward, not like the shy women they knew, and somehow or other invited themselves back to the hotel for "residents only" drinks. Sheila pulled James into a side street on the way to the lodgings; put a hand on his fly and her mouth on his lips. Aroused by the shock, James Downey gave in to her advances. With dishonourable intentions noted they ran past the others and into the hotel lobby. James felt all eyes on him. He was married with a young daughter. He was from a long line of devout Catholics. This was wrong, so wrong, but as he collected the room key James knew it was right for him for one night. He was a good-looking man and he was leaving tomorrow. Sheila was voracious. She controlled every vein in James' body. When he thought himself finished she roused him again, her mouth on his manhood, her cupped hand on his balls. He even attempted the priest-preferred position and with her, it was guilt free. "I've got to go, me ma will be waiting up – enjoy the rest of your stay and give my love to the boys back home." Her parting, like all her approaches, was honest and direct. James lay on in the bed wondering why Moira couldn't be more like her. The answer was simple. Sheila had been to a Convent.

Bathed in sunshine under the shadow of the Mournes such fond remembrances stirred James. Instantly aware of his whereabouts and the company he was keeping he stood up, turned his back on the group and put on his trousers. "I'll go and get the drinks, Moira."

"So soon?"

"Well, that way I'll miss the rush and besides I can get a paper. Right girls, what do you want?"

Before they had a chance to squint an answer, Moira Downey responded – "Get them orange squash, James and I'll have brown lemonade."

"OK, see you later." Still buttoning his shirt James Downey clambered up the rocks with boyish pride in his erection. "Can we go for a swim?" asked Marie, seizing the opportunity of paternal absence. She knew her mother would be unable to refuse, and soon the two girls were jumping in the icy water dodging bladder wrack and jellyfish.

As they shivered under their towels with Moira speed-patting their backs dry James returned with their drinks and by a quarter to twelve Kitty Tier's catering was once again under scrutiny. A fan of the Women's Institute Cookery Pamphlet, Kitty Tier was experimental with her sandwich fillings. Cooked ham, although fine for an evening salad, was too expensive at lunchtime. It took a lot to fill a Mother's Pride loaf so today's offerings were both interesting and cheap. Oonagh prised open a white triangle to gaze on a mixture of Plum rose chopped ham and tomato. Although she had no idea what dogs ate she thought this to be dog food and returned it to the waxed paper package. The tomato and salad cream was more to her liking. Marie devoured the cheese and apple triangles and watched as her mother carefully unwrapped each parcel giving the rounds that contained dog food to her father.

So, a daily routine was set; mornings beach, packed lunch, boating lake or pool, chips and a walk. Rain on the fifth day changed all that once again. *Typical,* thought Moira Downey, *Just as I was getting a wee bit of colour.* This utterance depressed everyone at breakfast. "It's on for the day," chirped Mrs Tier distributing her hot daily offerings. "Still, they say the weekend will be nice." This consoled few as many had only booked for the week. After the daily toilet run and coat collection they piled into the car and headed up the coast. James Downey was full of energy that day. They had a fish n' chips lunch in Rostrevor, his idea, they saw the Convent that Marie had escaped, most certainly his idea, and they ate ice creams in the car by the sea – definitely his suggestion. Moira went along with all of this, as she had the night before when his hand had raised her nightdress while the girls slept. She wouldn't let him do the 'dirty thing' and had remained on her back as he ploughed on. Thomas Cooper would never have suggested she turn over. He had been so considerate, so understanding for such a big man. Still, now that Marie had the eleven plus that was all over – probably for the best.

The rain eased off just in time for the Pierrots' evening performance. This was Moira's suggestion, soundly approved by all. Clutching rain macs as they took their seats all were nervous with excitement. The Downey's had told Oonagh so much about these summer entertainers that they feared she might be let down. As the man took their money and handed out blue numbered tickets the Downeys prayed that the show would live up to all their expectations. They need not have worried for Oonagh was already thrilled. No one had ever handed her a free ticket for anything.

As the Victorian bandstand lit up the damp holidaymakers cheered, the band took their seats and, to the strains of, "Oh I do like to be beside the seaside," the compere arrived on stage. At first Oonagh thought he looked like a fat Sean Teakle – but as he skipped around the stage, she changed her mind. Most of the audience – even Marie, knew all his jokes but that didn't seem to bother him. In fact he encouraged them to shout back at him and they laughed all the more because of it. He told jokes about his landlady, his mother-in-law and his daughter – even though James Downey was convinced that his mother was probably the only woman in his life. Perhaps he was a fat Sean Teakle after all. After a round of sing-a-long songs Albert Eccles, for that was the entertainer's name, announced the talent competition. You could enter by buying a pink ticket from Daisy and Masie – the pink-jacketed girls passing through the audience.

In unison Marie and Moira's hands shot into the air. Ever the pushy mother, Moira would make sure that her daughter would return to Belfast a star.

"What shall I sing?" asked Marie.

"Oh, give them Nobody's Child – that should do it." Oonagh was saddened that her special song was to be someone else's but was glad that the song thief was her best friend.

The talent contest was in the second half. Marie had to wait for the magician and the knife thrower to finish. During the interval, while Oonagh and James ate Moon Rockets Moira put Marie over her words. There wasn't that much talent, it wasn't that much of a contest. A fat boy from Fermanagh did three magic tricks assisted by his younger fatter sister, two pinched faced children, obviously cousins did some out of place ballroom dancing, three eight year olds did three year old Irish dancing and a spotty lad with glasses – too old for short trousers recited a poem by Percy Bysshe Shelley. Goaded by his mother, he teetered onto the stage. His enforced centre parting made him a comical figure and by tangling up the consonants in the author's name he rendered Bysshe Pish. The sniggering triggered by this lapse built in volume and forced him to abandon the performance mid verse – a slap on the back of the head his only maternal reward. He didn't return for the judging. He never returned to the Pierrots.

Contestants were lined up along the front of the stage. The applause of the audience was the decider. Albert Eccles walked behind the performers with a red cardboard arrow – as he lowered it over the contestant's head the audience clapped. Daisy and – in a well-rehearsed routine – leapt forward encouraging the audience with calls of 'we can't hear you'. Marie was the clear winner that night and, despite the all too obvious lack of competition Oonagh and the Downey parents beamed with pride.

"Isn't that just lovely?" said Mrs Tier as Moira made Marie display the trophy.

"You're lucky to have such a talented daughter."

"Indeed we are," smiled Moira Downey. "Indeed we are."

On the last day, the saddest day of the summer Oonagh and Marie shopped for souvenirs. Oonagh bought three postcards, a packet of talc-filled joke cigarettes and an ashtray for her non-smoking parents – after all, you never knew when people would drop in. Marie bought a bracelet for herself and a matching one for Oonagh, a brooch for her mother, a book of postcards and a matchbox holder for her Dad. After much deliberation in the shop near the Slieve Donard, Moira Downey purchased a lavender cardigan with imitation pearl buttons. It was soft, beautiful and expensive for a lavender cardigan with imitation pearl buttons. She asked for extra care and tissue in the wrapping and waited by the post box for the girls and her husband. James Downey spent his shopping time in the Castlewellan Arms – reading the Irish News and supping on a pint of Bass with a dash of lime. It was Declan Maguire's summer drink – so only fair that, on his insistence James should try it. Declan had left a note at 'Tall Trees' on the second day of their stay. He would have invited them all round to the parents but his father was poorly and that, coupled with the changeable weather made for an ill welcome for strangers. When in Newcastle Declan Maguire spent most of his mornings in the Castlewellan Arms – there were few Eileen's or Sheila's to entertain them here.

"One for the road?" enquired Declan returning from the urinal.

"Why not?" James replied. "Sure, we're on holiday."

It didn't feel like it given the ear bashing he received all the way from the post box to 'Tall Trees'. Moira didn't like drink and didn't like her husband meeting the likes of Declan Maguire. He was the road to no town that one. James Downey saw no presents until they returned to Belfast. It was as Moira Downey was in mid flow; just at the gates of 'Tall Trees' that Annie Slevin turned the corner.

"Hello Marie, hello Oonagh, what a lovely surprise."

Moira Downey, shocked by this sudden gust of fresh air, abandoned her scolding and stated the obvious, "Why Miss Slevin, how well you look."

She did indeed look well. Annie Slevin freed of her parents' old home and the constraints of the school system had spent the week at the Slieve Donard Hotel. Her aim had been to reflect on the past and to prepare for the grand tour ahead. London and Paris were on the agenda but Italy – land of love and song – was her goal.

"Thank you. I do hope you're enjoying your stay – all the best girls."

Awaiting neither reply nor acknowledgement Annie Slevin walked on to her hotel. She had nothing in common with these people; she'd abandoned the children for good. Like her, they must make their own way in the world. As the girls shouted a goodbye, their waving hands acknowledged with a slight turn of the head, James watched those Slevin hips twist along the path. If only he'd met a woman like her – assured and exhilarating, someone true and unpredictable. *If only I could be like her, thought Marie, off to sing my way round the world, without anyone telling me what to do. If only I could be like her, without responsibilities, free to pursue my heart,* thought Moira Downey. *Poor Miss Slevin,* thought Oonagh. *No husband and no parents and her with such lovely red hair.* Their thoughts unshared they entered Tall Trees for the last time. The end of the holiday had arrived.

Chapter Four

Oonagh loved her Saturday job in Anne's. She didn't know who Anne was for; Nuala, who owned the hairdressers, had thought it good for the business to keep the name of the previous proprietor. In a country where tradition is king this was a wise move. Oonagh's father knew the Magennis well and had put in a good word for his daughter but it was the girl's quiet demeanour and carefully braided hair that had won Nuala over. Their last Saturday girl was a terrible gossip and had been caught with her hand in the tea money jar so a vacancy was quickly created for 'a friend of the family'. The O'Callaghan parents hoped that the job would help fourteen year-old Oonagh out of her shell and them with pocket money. They could not have dreamt that it would kindle so much ambition in a girl so long devoid of hope.

It was a small salon, more a wee shop really, with a layout that had changed little since its opening. New floor tiles, two studded mirrors, a 'good-as-new' drier and a beaded curtain had been Nuala's only changes. Her sister Susan had added a corner table for the red phone and a red and gold book for appointments. Much of the book remained empty, as the regulars were so regular that all knew of their appointments and anyone else just dropped in and waited on one of the three seats by the window. The two sisters worked morning and night to make a go of it and were only too glad to welcome someone new 'onto the staff'.

The 'wee O'Callaghan girl' soon got to know the many foibles of their clients. How the Donaghy sisters always liked a currant square with their tea and only half a sugar each as they were trying to cut down. How Mrs Collins liked two magazines at a time – partly to deprive anyone else and partly so she wouldn't have to talk to Roisin Maguire who always came in for a cut and blow at the same time. How Aideen O'Connor always liked to hand over her church raffle money without anyone knowing in case they thought her a gambler. Between cups of tea and towel collection Oonagh brushed greying hair into the corner and put combs and scissors into the steriliser. Each Saturday she learned something new and the little brown envelope handed over always at six o'clock was just reward for her efforts.

In this tiled sanctuary Oonagh heard of shooting, kneecapping, the practise of tar and feathering. She also learned how to properly apply nail varnish, how to water down the shampoos, how to apply tint and how to do 'a tight wee set'. She was promoted to junior on leaving school and the little brown envelope grew a little fatter. Her grades were good but 'A' levels were not for her. A trade was more to her liking. Initially, her mother was disappointed – the Downey daughter was doing her 'A's' – but the extra money would help and with each little treat her disappointment lessened. Until marriage, Oonagh gave half her wages to her mother and saved the other half in a drawer with her pants.

Marie Downey was too busy for a Saturday job. Singing lessons and elocution took up the free time that wasn't occupied by baby-sitting her five-year-old brother. Miracle of miracles – James Downey and his wife had had another child – a boy, Niall Thomas Downey. All James efforts in Newcastle had hit home but although he tried and tried he could never get a little brother for Niall. Moira Downey was charmed by Niall. Marie was delighted – it let her off the hook. There was less checking upon her. Not that she did anything worth a check-up. Oonagh was the only person to keep tabs on Marie since the move to Holywood. Once Niall was born it was all change for the Downeys. James had been given a promotion – he was 'Head of Sales', whatever that meant, and a sense of doing better was not suited to their current neighbourhood. So with a characteristic optimism the Downeys mortgaged a home in Princess Gardens. Marie was transferred to the 'Sacred Heart' in the town. It was hidden behind laurel hedges, gated in black iron and not at all the proud establishment she had left. A new Catholic school in a community that embraced change and was fearful of it. The boys at the school next door were initially of interest but they had girls of their own and, like much of the town, kept themselves to themselves. Marie's elocution and singing classes grew in importance. On a good day, James Downey would transport her into and across town, but, he was away most of the time and on three days three buses or a bus and a black taxi were the only options.

For Marie, if the buses were under attack on the Andersonstown Road, the black taxis were the last resort. Anyone going in the same direction would pile into the illegal forms of transport. Anyone could brush up against Marie's suedette coat and breathe beer in her face. Still, the journey was worth it for Miss Kingan's hour-long singing lesson or Mrs Watts Drama Class.

With some of her Saturday money Oonagh would make a Wednesday night call to the Downey home. The girls chatted senselessly until the money ran out and once a month James Downey would collect Oonagh outside the hairdressers and bring her to their royal residence. It was always difficult collecting Oonagh, the corner shop was now enveloped in a control zone. James Downey regularly urged anyone in the household to come with him but often he had to make the journey alone and as no car could be left unattended he could only hope that a parking space was available outside the shop. It never was and so under English surveillance he would circle the block until the Saturday girl emerged. Oonagh loved those Saturdays at the Downeys. She'd style Marie's long red hair, tell her all about the salon (that's what she called it when in Holywood), put Marie over her words for the Poetry Society exams and hear her latest song recital. Everything in 22 Princess gardens was fresh and clean – Oonagh was careful not to leave any marks on the gloss white banisters as they were summoned downstairs for tea. Every visit was the same, every tea identical. As Niall Downey was reminded yet again to stop kicking chair legs Moira passed round white ham sandwiches. This was special ham, according to Moira Downey; it came from 'Larry's'. This made no impression on Oonagh as Larry was a stranger to her. If only she'd met him, they'd have got on well. He was a white haired butcher who loved the locals and knew their history. Equally loving chapel and chops he had a smile for every customer and a 'what about you' for all. Bells supplied the sausage rolls and mushroom patties (mini vol au vents oozing with creamed beige). This bakery just down from the Maypole gave Hollywood its sense of grandeur. Out front Mrs Bell, supplied wheaten scones, apple tarts and celebration cakes but if you went through a glass door at the back of the shop – a new world opened out; a long counter with bar stool seating on one side, three three-seater tables at the other. Here, Maudie served up Cornish pasties, meat and potato pies, tart and custard to bank managers and secretaries on weekdays and to schoolchildren and their parents at weekends.

The mushroom patties, alien initially, were Marie's favourites – preferring savoury to sweet, she loved the quaint sophistication and vowed to have them when she got married. Oonagh saved a space for the lemon cake that followed. The girls slept in Marie's room when the talk ran out. With boys, fashion, make up and their dreams to discuss – their eyes closed only briefly. The monthly Saturday pattern was broken only once. Oonagh left school at Easter and had accepted Nuala's offer of a permanent position; a double cause for celebration according to Marie, as on that Wednesday she won her class at Holywood Festival and had been asked to compete for the prestigious Sanctus Boscus award on the Gala Night. Naturally she invited Oonagh, who, since she didn't start full time till Tuesday, jumped at the chance.

That Friday lunchtime journey across town was very stressful. Oonagh had left home in good time, her overnight bag crammed with heated rollers, styling brushes and a secret bottle of Mateus Rose for celebration. The red bus into town was diverted and she arrived at the City Hall flustered. She walked down past Anderson and McAuley, Mays Jewellers and crossed the road at the law courts. That way she avoided the security barriers and having to have her bag searched. Sirens blared out and land rovers patrolled the streets. Oonagh wasn't frightened, she worked near the city centre after all, this was her town and no bloody incident could stop her being with her friend. She arrived at Oxford Street bus station, purchased some toffetts from the hatch at the entrance and hunted out the correct stand.

The Ulster bus depot was quiet that lunchtime and Oonagh started munching on her chocolate-coated toffees long before the blue and cream bus arrived. 'Bangor via Holywood' was its destination and Oonagh asking for the Holywood Post Office, paid the driver and sat down by the window. Five minutes later she was on her way. For Oonagh this was another world. She clutched her bag tightly on her lap and spoke to no one. Nervous as the bus halted on the Albert Bridge Road she tried not to stare at the woman with two children who boarded. She probably lived in one of those red-handed terraces that longed to 'kick the Pope'. Oonagh was glad she'd decided against the drop earrings that gave too much away. Along the Old Holywood Road Oonagh looked from Holywood Hills to Palace Barracks, freedom to oppression in one gaze – that was Northern Ireland for you. She was glad to step down off the bus and greet her friend. Marie had been outside the Post office for ages – trying not to look suspicious.

They went to Bells for two meat and potatoes and two cokes. Marie was still in her uniform as she'd been competing that morning. Naturally, she'd won the sonnet class so she was a bit full of herself, thought Oonagh. "Well done Marie," said a craggy faced woman waiting for two Cornish pasties – one for her and one for her greasy haired son. Mrs Sprowl was offering consolation for his coming second to 'that wee Downey girl' whose presence in Bells was adding insult to injury. The pies were far too hot, which explained Maudie's tea-clothed handling of them, and between mouthfuls and hushed catch up sentences the girls blew on their forks to render the food edible.

Marie paid, Moira Downey had given her the money, and the two friends headed off on foot to Princess Gardens. Because of the Festival Marie had the whole day off and she was looking forward to Oonagh's help with performance preparation.

"Did you have a nice lunch?" asked Mrs Downey ushering them into the hall.

"Lovely, thank you Mrs Downey," replied Oonagh

"I'm just popping out for some messages and to collect Niall. Marie, have you told Oonagh all about tonight? It's so exciting."

Moira closed the back door behind her and the girls could breathe again.

Chapter Five

Holywood Festival was the old guard at play. Chaired, and indeed run, by a retired army major whose family had been in linen, it had featured in the North Down social calendar since 1950. The promotion of music and drama was purported to be its focus but in truth much of its raison d'être was to give the major something to do. He needed people to command and who better than the aspiring middle classes born and bred in this trouble free haven. His Anglo-Irish upbringing, and his time in the Army enforced the Major's unionism and the gala night was a chance to display Ulster at its best. The committee members, all approved by him, were his soldiers of art, their ranks denoted by silk embroidered badges. General ranks had green badges, red for Adjudicator's badges, blue for the Secretary, yellow for the Treasurer and cream for the Chairman; all proudly pinned these to their chest vowing to uphold the Major's values. He rallied local regiments of cake bakers, ministers and publicans alike. In days of non-sponsorship he gained sponsors and when the funds were low a cheque from a mystery donor would soon swell them. All knew the identity of the mystery sponsor but the committee members, loyal to a woman, kept the Major's little secret to themselves.

The Adjudicator, always English, was billeted in the Windsor Hotel. Situated near the Palace Barracks, this establishment had no royal connections but, despite that, the Toner family made sure their mainland guests felt quite at home. The pre festival wine and cheese parties were held there; fundraisers for the festival, where hard cubes of cheddar were washed down with bitter Beaujolais. There was no finesse in the choice of cheese or wine and the baguette, so popular now, was regarded as a foreign delicacy. On her first trip to France, Saint Brieuc by coach, Marie had purchased six giant bread batons for her Holywood home. Her parents had been thrilled and, despite the stale nature of the produce – the baguettes having hardened on the two-day boat and coach trip – they dipped blocks of bread in their gifted café au lait bowls and pretended the French really had something. Marie was saddened to see the well-travelled bread sticks in the dustbin the following day. At least she'd tried to bring a little culture to Princess Gardens. Surely stale culture was better than no culture at all?

The Major shared Moira's view, and he rallied local shopkeepers, forced conversation in the library, made policemen stand to attention – anything to make sure his finest hour, the Gala night was a success. Protestant and Catholic families of note heard his rallying cries and purchased tickets for the gala supper well in advance. Moira Downey thought it fitting that she do likewise. It was their fourth year in Holywood, time to be integrated. She purchased the tickets at the start of the week but with Marie gaining a free competitor pass they had one spare. James Downey had instigated the Oonagh invitation; both Moira and her daughter were initially uncertain, "I doubt if it's really her thing."

"Nonsense Marie, besides she could do your hair."

"Oh I suppose so. Why not?" She's getting just like her mother thought James and instantly reprimanded himself for the thought.

All afternoon Oonagh worked at Marie's hair. She heated the rollers as Marie watched but there was little consultation – this client knew exactly what she wanted – in fact she had cut out several examples from 'Jackie' to make sure Oonagh didn't get it wrong. Mrs Downey had leant them her giant can of Ellnette hair spray. They were taking the car to the Queen's Hall and nothing would be out of place on their arrival.

With Marie's thick red hair the flicked back look was hard to achieve. Oonagh was sure a cut was essential but she hadn't learned how to do that yet and didn't want to show herself up. She struggled masterfully with spray and rollers – teasing squirting, occasionally swearing and finally she achieved Marie's approval.

Marie chose a pale blue eye shadow and sugary pink lipstick to complete the look. She'd bought them in Fresh Garbage – a hippy chic shop that smelled of incense, patchouli and body odour. Oonagh was jealous of the long Etam dress that Marie produced from the wardrobe. Half Laura Ashley, half New Seekers', it fitted her perfectly and the pale blue and lemon flowers clung to her fine frame in all 'the right' places.

She added some ropes of love beads and two blue and yellow bangles and the look was complete. Pale blue suede ankle-strapped sandals with a medium wedge gave her additional height. Moira had bought them in Lily and Skinner at the weekend as a good luck charm. She'd never be able to wear them into Belfast. People wearing similar had lost their soles as security guards searched for explosives. Who would ruin a beautiful shoe for a terrorist act? Had these people no idea? Explosives in a shopping bag, a car, a pram, yes – but not in a suede wedge.

Oonagh squirted some more spray, teased the hardened fluids with a tail comb and stood back to admire her friend.

"Ready girls?" How the time had flown. They heard the keys in the door, the parental preparations and the arrival of Amy, from across the road, to baby-sit.

"Shit," said Oonagh – lost in her friend's transformation she'd neglected her own. Rummaging in her bag for her brown trouser suit, she thought how typical this was. Marie was always the centre of attention – even for her. Scraping her hair back with a piece of brown velvet ribbon she pulled the white turtleneck jumper over her head and donned the sleeveless jerkin. Glad she'd worn her two-tone brown boots on the bus; she pulled on the wide legged pants and adjusted her top. "Here, borrow this, it'll brighten it up." Oonagh wasn't at all sure about the long orange beads and the three plastic bangles but Marie was probably right. She had an eye for detail. Orange was probably fine here in Holywood – she'd never have got away with it at home or the hairdressers for that matter. The room was a mess, the girls rushed downstairs. "Don't you look lovely," smiled Mrs Downey, obviously talking solely about her daughter. She beamed back an acknowledgement as she said, "So do you mother."

Moira Downey did indeed look lovely. She was wearing a black and white checked cape with huge velvet buttons and a velvet collar, a white straw hat with a black satin band and black and white woven sling backs. Oonagh gazed in awe and wondered how they would fit into the car. Checking herself in the narrow hall mirror, Moira Downey aerosoled all in Lanvin Arpege and led the procession to the car.

Suddenly remembering herself, she turned and whispered loudly – a stage whisper fine tuned during rehearsals for 'Lock up your Daughter' – to Amy, "We shouldn't be that late – make sure he's in bed by eight," Amy nodded. She'd spend the evening on the phone and pay Niall to lie.

If getting into the Citroen saloon was a palaver, getting out was almost a disaster. A gust of May wind threatened to remove Mrs Downey's crowning glory and if Marie hadn't had the presence of mind to don a chiffon scarf in the car all Oonagh's work would have been ruined. They'd parked at the corner of Church View so it was only a small walk to the Queen's Hall.

Past the Golden Age Club and the row of terraced houses where the mad woman lived, across the zebra crossing at Kearney's Children's outfitters – where protestant grammar school pupils bought their uniforms and left after the fire station. Oonagh, clutching a bag for touch ups, was glad they didn't go as far as the Orange Hall. James Downey presented the tickets at the door and Oonagh and Marie went off to regain perfection.

The hall was opposite the council chambers so the Queen greeted all as they climbed the stairs. She wasn't there in person – not even the Major could sort that but this oil painting was treated with so much respect that she might as well have been.

Under its tired gilt frame the Downeys' waited for the girls. All four entered the hall together. James, as instructed in the bedroom by his wife, bought two programmes. They were all here, the Blaneys, he was a Doctor, she was a bohemian, the Hunts, he was a businessman, she was a teacher, the Delaneys and the Fogartys, the Toners and the O'Connors. Allied to their respective teachers of speech and song they sat, as in church, hypocritically seeking attention.

Mirrored by their protestant counterparts – they longed for ecumenical solutions but made sure they sat on the right side of the adjudicator.

Miss Lennon, a committee member or so it said on her badge, approached Marie Downey.

"Mary Downey?" she inquired

"Marie," smiled Moira.

"Oh sorry, Marie. You're performing tonight as winner of the Dunn Cup, the Shakespeare trophy and the Linehan shield – is that right? That entitles you to compete for our prestigious Sanctus Boscus award. Would you mind sitting at the front with the other competitors?"

"Oh OK," smiled Marie as she was ushered away.

Once again, Oonagh found herself stuck with Mr Downey.

His wife, realising Marie couldn't sit with them had moved along to be with Marie's teachers, Miss Kingan, song mistress, Mrs Watt, speech and drama doyenne.

James was glad he'd held on to one of the programmes', that way he could follow the proceedings and would have something to say to the O'Callaghan girl if needed. He was relieved that his wife had moved – he found her nervousness exhausting. He had no desire to be accepted in Holywood for he knew they'd never accept a travelling salesman. Born in the town – you may just have had a chance – but with no local connections you were at a disadvantage. He implored his wife to be happy with her lot but she longed for people to stare at her at mass and comment on their success. Stare they would but out of pity. Moira Downey was determined to be accepted by this town and her daughter's inherited talents, or so she believed could help her do just that.

From her new position of power she gazed back at her husband. James always sided with the underdog – he was always seen in the wrong company. She beckoned him to join her but he assured her that they were fine where they were. Despairing of him, yet again, she smiled at the adjudicator and returned to study the programme. The smile was duly noted by the adjudicator steward and two committee members. It wasn't done – the adjudicator must remain impartial – smiling was forbidden. The Downey woman showed no respect for tradition, rules or regulations. A pushy Belfast catholic – no wonder the town was going to the dogs.

Oonagh was glad she'd worn trousers. The seat was hard metal and bentwood with an inconsiderate hole at the back. She was glad of a vacant seat beside her so she could keep an eye on her bag. They may be posh, but were they too posh to pinch? At seven o'clock sharp thundering applause ushered a small grey haired woman onto the stage. Dwarfed by two floral displays she struggled to be seen. Being heard was not a problem.

Years of elocution lessons had given the Festival secretary the voice of a well-worn church bell. In a resonant tone she bellowed welcomes to lords, ladies and gentlemen, thanked everyone for a marvellous week, painfully described 'the Sanctus Boscus' award and recommended tea in the cloisters during the interval.

Oonagh wanted to laugh but as everyone around her sat stony-faced she realised this was how things were done in Holywood and kept her eyes on the floor and her laughter to herself.

Her annual performance applauded the secretary welcomed the major who, having struggled with a vase of peonies, declared the gala evening open. The grey haired and suited lady then reappeared from the Forest of Arden and announced the winners onto the stage; all were competing for the coveted 'Holy Wood' award – a cheque for twenty five pounds – one for music and one for speech and drama to go towards tuition. The Major, having been through Sandhurst, believed education to be worth fighting for.

Boredom enveloped Oonagh long before Marie took to the stage. She had no notion why someone should be praised for speaking like an English person. Even W.B. Yeats suffered at protestant hands. Marie was good at the sonnets, but under pressure she fluffed her Shakespeare. Oonagh was sure she heard Mrs Downey tut her disapproval. Lady Macbeth was not Marie. The only stain she'd ever wash away was that left by Thomas Cooper on her suede coat all those years ago. She was an unconvincing murderess and Oonagh was sure that the greasy Sprowl would steal it with his Richard III. Given his demeanour it was not so much acting merely time travel. The violin and piano winners were impressive but Marie's Celtic song selection, sung in English of course won the heart of Ian Godfrey and on presenting Marie with her cheque and plaque he revealed that even the English can have an Irish past – his grandmother had come from County Donegal.

George Sprowl did indeed win the drama award. As was customary, yet painful, the competitors congratulated each other. If only Marie had been more like the Scottish lady she'd have pierced him with her plaque. The daggers from the eyes of the Downey matriarch were wound enough. How good that a

47

Presbyterian should win with Shakespeare, reflected Mrs Sprowl – these Catholics were better off with their diddly-dee. Mrs Blaney overheard the twisted observation – glad that a Sprowl, who obviously lacked any musical talent, would never dabble in her culture.

Oonagh was delighted for her friend but there was little room for her in the celebrations. If she'd felt ill at ease during the concert she was completely lost at the Gala Supper. The Toners had gone to town. There was chicken fricassee, paprika beef, roast ham, rice salads all displayed on oblong tables with heated stands and plates. Dressed Pimms was paraded on silver trays around the room and then – at a given signal – the major stood up, called everyone to attention and gave one final traditional order – "Ladies, trifles forward."

At that precise moment the doors of the function room flew open and a flotilla of hostess gowned committee members entered all proudly carrying before them a homemade trifle. Neither the Downeys nor Oonagh had ever seen birds' custard treated with such reverence. Marie knew of the importance of the haggis for the Scottish – perhaps trifle was the same for the good burgers of Hollywood. Needing to fit, Moira Downey encouraged them all to applaud the procession. Marie spent the whole evening being congratulated on her singing; her confidence and her appearance but the defeat by the Sprowl had unsettled her. No man would ever get the better of her again. That night Oonagh listened as Marie talked. She had plans, she had new friends, and she would be a success. The Gala evening had proved that and, as Oonagh boarded the early bus into town she sensed that this would be her last visit to Holywood. Moira Downey didn't like her, James Downey had hardly said two words to her and Marie – well, she was just Marie.

Chapter Six

Michael Truesdale drove his white Austin Marina through the second UDR checkpoint of the evening. He knew a couple of the lads defending Ulster but he still got annoyed at having to stop for them. He wanted to get to the gig before the new girl went on stage, for Michael prided himself on two things – his talent coaching skills and his punctuality. The new Holywood by-pass helped him arrive at the Queen's Court in ample time to find a parking space and apply a little Paco Rabane to his flustered cheeks. Hurriedly placing the dark green canister of pee-yellow liquid in the glove compartment, Michael rummaged for the yellow Krooklok and clamped it to the steering wheel of his proudest possession. This was not much of a criminal deterrent but the newness of the car had encouraged extra caution. Just because the white vehicle had 'only one previous owner' there was no need to abandon it. He clunked the Krooklok tight, locked the driver's door and approached the hotel. The Queen's Court Hotel could never live up to its title. This peeling white building off the high Street once had rooms and holidaymakers but now it was barely two bars and a dance floor. The clientele – off duty soldiers and school-leavers hoped to enter into a short-term Anglo-Irish agreement – sex in one of the many entries that ran between the terraces of shops and houses. This was no ballroom of romance. Policed by three bald headed security guards it was a safe haven for those who intended to escape from the fear of attack.

Few civilians socialised in Belfast. It was a ghost town. Since the Abercorn Restaurant bombing five years earlier people were cautious of city centre nightspots. They needed to socialise on their doorsteps and Michael Truesdale – ever the entrepreneur – had seen yet another business opportunity. He had set up a small agency to help local businesses find acts that were prepared to travel. His approach was simple. He promised the acts a full summer of bookings but refused to reveal the venues until they were signed up. Of course this was a bit of a gamble but with so many sectarian protection rackets and paramilitary enlisted venues – all talent needed an insider. Michael Truesdale had a foot in both camps. He knew everyone yet kept himself to himself. The product of a mixed marriage – he could play either game – to some he was the most catholic of Catholics, to others a truly protestant-protestant. He always said nothing or just the right thing. He gave little away but always got what he wanted at the right price.

"Hello Davey – how are you?"

"Ah, can't complain," grunted the bald-headed security guard. "Your lot are all in. That wee girl's some looker."

"Aye, she is."

With this curt acknowledgement, Michael passed the toilets and walked down the sticky carpeted steps into the ballroom.

The country show band was still setting up. Marie Downey sat nervously on some steps at the side of the stage. How she wished that they'd hurry up. She'd only had a couple of front room rehearsals with them. This was her first proper gig – had they no consideration. Besides, her mother and father were coming to hear her. This wasn't their usual place of entertainment so she at least would have to be perfect. Michael had kindly organised two tickets for them and had reserved a banquette near the stage. It was good to have someone so mature take an interest.

"So, M, how's it going?" Marie knew this was Michael Truesdale long before she heard the words. The squeak of his crepe-soled shoes on the parquet and the overpowering odour of Paco Rabane gave him away.

"Good so far I think – we're behind in the setting up, have still got to do the sound check, there's no ironing board in the dressing room and Spud-u-like 'ran out of potatoes'."

"That's shocking, kid!" smiled Michael.

He'd first met Marie in a pub in Kilburn. She was with a group of musicians whom he didn't notice much. It was her performance of the 'Fields of Athenry' that held his attention. This girl was sun kissed, innocent and beautiful. Sure she was young, but surely that was an advantage. She was thrilled as he presented her with his card. "Michael Truesdale – Star Manager Star Agent." Over a snowball or two she'd explained that she shouldn't really be in the bar. She wasn't yet eighteen. Her friends and she were going back to Belfast after a summer of community exchange holidays on the west coast of France. This was their last night in London before they split up.

"So where are you off to, Marie Downey?"

"Back home to Ireland, Belfast to finish my A's."

"And then what?"

"Oh the parents want me to go to Queens – so probably that."

"Well, should you ever fancy making a bit of money singing – I'm your man – give me a call when you hit the homeland."

She'd called six months later and here they were.

The manager didn't stay for the whole sound check; he listened to three songs, gave Marie some notes on mic technique, eye contact with the audience and checked out what she was wearing. Mission accomplished – he went off on foot round Bangor. While Davey kept an eye on the car, Michael Truesdale had a drink with Big Steve at the Royal hotel, an argument with Jerry at the Hillside Bar and a few words of advice for Margot – the drag act hosting the variety night at the Lansdowne Court. He bought a pastie and chip from Mr Chip and sat down to enjoy his tea. As he wiped his greasy fingers on the dull white paper he gazed out towards Pickie Pool. His kids would never play there – they'd have something much better than ice-cold water in a small town.

Despite blanket protests and control zones, no go areas and occasional curfews his business was thriving. All over the north his acts were prospering and earning their keep. He hadn't lost any of them and aimed to keep it that way. 'M' could be a real money-spinner if she kept at it. She had Irish charm and English sophistication and boy could she sing – if only he was a bit younger. He finished the last of his chips and went back to the Queen's Court to check on the sales.

Moira Downey wasn't sure about the Queen's Court. She'd read awful things about it in the County Down Spectator. There were always fights and cases of illegal alcohol sales to minors reported in the court section. Of course it couldn't possibly be like the shabeens that had sprung up all over west Belfast but as Moira also considered the people of Bangor 'common' there was probably little difference. James thought Michael Truesdale's offer of tickets very considerate. After all, it wasn't a real night out. James couldn't remember when they'd last had a proper one of those, as Niall was still far too young to be left on his own. The offer of something free, however, was irresistible and it was to hear their daughter after all. He organised for Niall to sleep over at a friend's house so Moira would have no excuse.

They'd decided against taking the car so when a taxi pulled up at the allotted time the neighbours were all agog. They didn't speak to the neighbours on the left hand side of the drive. To be precise – the neighbours had never spoken to them. The Magowans, for that was the name of the silent trio at no 20, believed Catholics to be a lower life form. Each July they'd goaded them with the hoisting of a union flag and the planting of Sweet William and orange lilies – all staunch reminders of a bigoted heritage.

Typical of their lot, thought Elaine Magowan, *getting a taxi when they've got that flash car blocking the road.*

Elaine Magowan walked everywhere. They had a car but only for special occasions. She watched the 'two taigs from next door' strut down the driveway and get into the hired car.

Moira Downey could feel narrow protestant eyes burrow into her back. She'd grown used to the pain over the years, hurt more for Niall than for herself. The Magowans' boy was a year older than her son and yet they never played together. She'd found it hard to explain why Ross Magowan didn't want to play – ever. She'd refused to adopt the easy tribal approach and could neither make sense of it for herself or out of it for her offspring.

James gave it little thought. The Magowans, to him suffered a sickness – an illness that could prevent them from ever being happy and whose only cure even lay within them.

The taxi driver was surprised when Moira Downey uttered the destination. They simply didn't look the type. His surprise increased when Moira proudly told them why they were going. Perhaps the couple weren't all that they seemed. He knew better than to ask questions or to continue the conversation. He'd also learned to slow down at checkpoints, hand over the car when first asked and to look out for number one.

Moira Downey hated having her bag searched at the Queen's Court by a fat bald man who called her love. Since Niall's birth she hated anyone poking through her things. She seldom went into Belfast now. She couldn't abide the body searches.

Once down the stairs she soon forgot these 'infringements of civil rights' when greeted by a suave gentleman oozing confidence and an unfamiliar scent.

"Mr & Mrs Downey – delighted you could come. I'm Michael Truesdale – M's manager."

"Oh hello," said Mrs Downey. "Thank you," added James. Moira Downey, despite the surroundings, thought the acquisition of such a manager a clever move. Marie had a talent and although the family believed in her they had no connection in the business; – a manager like Mr Truesdale obviously had.

No one paid more attention to the band that night than Marie Downey. No one paid more attention to Marie than Michael Truesdale. No one paid more attention to Michael Truesdale than Moira Downey. As the front table sipped vodka lime and sodas, the drink of the moment Marie prepared her set. She was enjoying every minute of it. OK so the clients were too busy trying to cop off to applaud but Marie knew she was doing a good job. She could see it in the eyes of her manager and her mother. Her mixture of pop and country was a winner and as she left the stage, she'd found her true calling.

In the dingy room that they called a dressing room Moira and James beamed with joy. This was their daughter. All those years of tuition had been worth it. She could hold her own on stage after all.

They kissed her goodnight – made sure she was alright for a lift home, and found the 'value cab' that had brought them. After he'd divided up the money – and counted the division several times, Michael Truesdale drove Marie home. At the bottom of the Croft road, just below the old people's home they pulled into a lay-by. Michael switched off the engine. "You were great tonight, well done." He leaned over to kiss her and found his hand caressing her thigh. Marie let him, stretching out on the brown leather seat to help his journey of discovery. Beneath her parents' home she returned the compliment – nervously rubbing her had ante clockwise round his crotch. He'd have to give her notes if her performance was to improve offstage, but not tonight. Tonight a snog and a damp fumble was enough.

"You were really, really great." Always in control Michael Truesdale re-started the car and deposited Marie Downey outside her parents'. "Always leave them wanting more" – that was his motto and, to date, it had never failed him. Marie's appetite grew and grew that summer. As she toured the province with 'Country Sound' Michael Truesdale was never far away. From Wedding receptions at Slieve Donard to young Farmers' dances in Five mile town they travelled in a rusty white van full of equipment accompanied by a white Austin Marina. Marie's confidence grew and travelling from gig to gig she learnt both new songs and independence. Naturally, her mother worried – although the campaign had switched to the mainland shootings were on the increase. Michael Truesdale did much to calm the Downey matriarch and it was a comfort indeed when Michael asked James Downey for his daughter's hand in marriage. The age difference was a bit of a sticking point but Marie had always been old beyond her years and after much pleading from their daughter the parents gave in. Moira was somewhat relieved when Marie's grades failed to get her a place at Queen's. The party line was that Marie had changed her mind – as the university was fast becoming a DUP stronghold. Funny, how the occupants of 20 Princess Gardens believed it a hot bed of republicanism. Maire's singing earned her money. Money gave her freedom. At last she could escape her mother's watchful eye, she could purchase ready to wear and develop her own style. Ironic, that by becoming an independent woman she was to capture a husband who felt delighted in control.

Wedding plans fitted around the summer gigs – much to Moira Downey's dismay. They were to be married at Easter in St Philip and St James – a pleasing church of the wrong denomination that looked down on some of Holywood's occupants. Moira Downey was initially distraught – her daughter was abandoning the faith of her mother but as she reflected on her carefree days in an orange Skoda which she'd hidden from James she grew to admire her daughter's courage and admiration turned to acceptance.

James Downey had spent so much time on the road that he cared little for his daughter's religious conviction. Lacking any himself, he only wished her happy.

Michael and Marie had paid the deposit for the reception at La Mon House but a February bombing resulted in the loss of the venue and twelve civilians. The Downey's had never been sure of Michael's choice of location and this merely proved them right. James and Moira threw caution to the wind for once and upgraded to a reception at the Culloden Hotel. As a wedding present Country Sound played for nothing and as the newlyweds drove off to Portstewart for the honeymoon Moira knew her daughter had, yet again, done the right thing.

Marie and Michael decided against children. With all the artists they looked after they had enough adolescents to care for. Michael preferred Marie's breasts when she was on the pill and, always wishing to please him, she was seldom off it. She toured with Country Sound for the first two years of their marriage but her new home needed attention so regular gigs became occasional and occasional meant 'only for friends'. Michael didn't mind. Truesdale's agency had really taken off and what with disco dancers, magicians, female impersonators and bands of all persuasions he needed someone in the office. Marie was the obvious candidate. Marie was the only person in the business that he trusted.

Their new home on Derryvolgie Avenue was perfect for such an arrangement. They'd moved there after two years in Ladas Drive. It was a huge step up and much to Moira Downey's liking. Marrying a protestant certainly did have its' advantages.

Concealed behind some elm trees, in a tree-lined avenue near the police station number forty-two was too large for two. Peopled often with Truesdale clients it became a drop-in-centre for showbiz counselling.

Marie could 'talk them up', give them a reality check, 'hear stories of rivalry' and 'swear herself to secrecy'. The office was downstairs on the left opposite the drawing room. It was only ever used for entertaining and at Christmas. The clients seldom saw it – their view of forty-two was a tiled porch, a peach and black office and an eau-de-nil loo if they'd come on foot.

Because Marie had been 'in the business' the turns loved her. They told her everything and this knowledge, shared with her husband, kept 'Truesdales' ahead of the game.

Michael spent much time away from home – checking out new venues, visiting virgin acts, and laundering money. Marie worried about the frequent border crossings, the journey's through Armagh, his phone call forgetfulness. She made a huge fuss of him on his return. Setting the mahogany table with the Kings silver and rustling up a chicken casserole. On these occasions her mother's phone line was an essential ingredient. Moira Downey could talk her daughter through every stage of a recipe – from shop to table. Home economics had never been Marie's forte and Moira was glad to do anything for a happy marriage – as long as it belonged to someone else.

Under this tutelage, Marie mastered the art of the Duchesse Potato and Cauliflower Mornay. Michael always praised her efforts – even if a fish supper was more to his liking. The neighbours kept themselves to themselves. Marie didn't care; her upbringing in Princess Gardens had prepared her for that. Class, not religion was the divide here. She was a former resident singer at the Conway Hotel and there was no getting away from that. Of course she was good morning'd at the parade of local shops but there were no drink invitations and no fondue parties. The Truesdale world was small, the extended Truesdale family large.

During the day Marie fielded calls, noted every transaction and kept the Truesdale Turns in positive mood. Michael did all the deals himself and made sure of two catch up days at home. These were always Marie's favourites. They were a great wee team. She'd answer the telephone, check if he was in and hand over the receiver. She was soft and charming; he was tough and business-like. Such a combination soon filled the booking sheets. An annual holiday in the South became two weeks in Spain. That in turn gained a weekend in Paris and Easter in Rome.

Once a month the Downeys came for Sunday lunch and Marie returned to Princess Gardens every two weeks. Marie always cooked a roast beef, her mother a stuffed pork fillet. Both supplied the customary vegetables – carrot and parsnip, potatoes – both roast and creamed and a seasonal green something, beans, peas or cabbage. Their lives, more regimented than humdrum were full. They were unworried by the Troubles; they had things to look forward to.

Monday evenings were Marie's favourites. Michael, unofficially, took Mondays off. Weekends were his busiest time and so Monday for him was his day of rest. Moira Downey often remarked on his frequent Sunday absences. Her husband observing that it was 'just part of the job' in a futile attempt to silence her.

On Monday evenings, Michael and Marie would curl up on the sofa, have a TV dinner and not talk about work. Eight years into their childless marriage, on a Monday like any other, 'Scene around Six' brought Marie's childhood back into her life.

"Police have released the names of those killed in Saturday's bomb attack the bus station…"

Marie was barely paying attention but something about the murdered father and son seemed familiar. She reached over and dialled her mother – "Yes, Marie, isn't it awful, poor Oonagh, what a terrible, terrible thing…"

She saw a gilt-edged wedding invitation on her mother's mantelpiece. She saw Sean O'Dwyer's name next to Oonagh O'Callaghans. She'd sent a set of knives 'no bloody use to anyone now'. She'd gone to France.

They'd lost touch. Did Oonagh still work at the hairdressers – what the hell was it called? Did her mother live in the same street? How would she contact her after all this time? As her mother lamented Marie's guilt grew. They hadn't fallen out, they'd just moved apart. She must get to Oonagh; she must be there for her friend.

Her mother was of no help. She'd moved to Holywood and severed all ties with the past. No one in St Agnes' knew the O'Callaghans – they weren't performers. She would have to do her own detective work.

Uneasily she slept. What were they doing at the bus station? Was Oonagh with them? Had she been injured? Was she lying at death's door in the Mater? Why had Sean O'Dwyer taken his seven-year-old son there? Did they still worship in the same parish? These questions troubled her all evening and in the morning, having kissed Michael off on a two-day trip she set about finding answers.

She started with the telephone directory flicking through its pages for clues. Discretion prevented her from calling anyone named O'Dwyer. Houses in mourning seldom take calls and the eight-year absence would make communication difficult. After a morning of confused frustration she gave up. The death notices would provide the information needed – she would offer her condolences in person. Her loss was true and the telephone, an instrument for daily lies was not the means of reconciliation.

Chapter Seven

Anne's was a haven for Oonagh; a place where she could achieve. She learnt to cut, set, perm and style and Nuala Maginnis grew to depend on her. When Susan went off to have her third baby, Oonagh took her chair. She was a stylist – and the nearest to one that Anne's Hairdressers had ever seen. A rise in wages and her own pair of scissors were the outside rewards, but the inner – Oonagh's growth, was unquantifiable.

She was confident at last. As her client numbers swelled she became more daring and when Nuala's cousin asked her out to his works 'do' she accepted.

'Sean O'Dwyer' was what her mother called 'a decent big fella'. He'd been to St Patrick's and had a steady job in Lynch's Bar in the city centre. One Friday he popped round to the salon with some keys for Nuala and there he saw Oonagh struggling with a demi-wave. He watched her twist brittle hair on a fine spindle and noted her beautiful nails against the roller. Sean, like most who'd attended a catholic all boys' school, was all boys. Shy around women he had no idea who to ask to the staff bash. Nuala had suggested Oonagh and it was a relief to him and everyone in the shop when she said yes.

Six months later, when he proposed, a second yes was an equal relief. The wedding was a family affair; a large batch of O'Dwyers and Magennis and a small contingent of O'Callaghans. Oonagh was annoyed that Marie didn't come – oh, they'd rushed things because of the baby, but a trip to France was no excuse and a set of knives no substitute for friendship. She knew they'd grown apart since the Holywood move but had sent the invite just in case she'd been wrong. She'd sent a thank you note with the slab of cake but received no acknowledgement. What with the wedding, then the baby, she didn't give it a second thought.

They were a happy trio – Oonagh, Sean and little Declan. Oonagh was guilty that he was looked after by Mrs O'Dwyer but as Sean said, "We need the money and at least you see him in the evenings."

Oonagh loved her life. Wednesdays were her favourites. The salon closed in the afternoon and so she and Sean could meet for lunch. He'd wheel Declan into the salon for the clients to chuckle at him with envy and for Nuala to give him some shiny coins and then this happy family could set off to either 'the Chalet d'or' or the Skandia. Both establishments welcomed children and served thin chips so both men in Oonagh's life were happy.

That Saturday, when all happiness ceased, was warm. July was often changeable but this year the heat was oppressive. Four had collapsed during the orange parade and red faces were everywhere. As Oonagh left for work Sean and the seven-year-old Declan planned their day out. Sean started work at five so he promised to leave Declan back at the salon on his way to the bar. Oonagh hoped to be able to slope off early as the hot weather meant the afternoons were slack. Besides, Susan owed her a few hours as she'd covered for her two weeks in a row.

The lads' plan was to go fishing in Bangor – down by Pickie pool. They'd get a bus from the city centre and have chips for lunch. They'd wanted to go by train but a Dublin derailment had thrown the network into chaos and Sean thought the buses more reliable.

Oonagh was so jealous. The heat of the salon was bad at the best of times but a busy morning with driers at full pelt had turned it into a sauna. Her pale lemon strappy top clung to her – a bargain from the sale it was an annoyance that she really didn't need.

Mrs Donaghy's set was annoyance enough. It simply wouldn't take. This problem wasn't new but no one in Anne's appeared to have a solution.

Eileen Donaghy was born with difficult hair. Since Anne's belonged to Anne she'd had it permed once a month and set every other Saturday but it was still obstinate. Oonagh had tried every style but the hair was as tough as its owner and, no matter what was created, it always went back to what it knew. In the black vinyl chair, wrapped in a cape of nylon Eileen Donaghy waited for Oonagh to do her best. She was going through 'the change and the tablets she was on were largely responsible for the brittle helmet she called a hairstyle. Oonagh put the last pin in the smallest roller. Scooped Mrs Donaghy into plastic ear protectors and a pink mesh net and trapped her under the drier to ferment.

At last she could have a fag. The girls nipped outside to smoke – only the customers could smoke on the premises. The red plastic ashtrays were reserved for them.

No sooner had she lit up than two girls from Divis arrived for a quick wash and blow. Susan and Nuala were both in tint mode and so the girls fell to Oonagh. Maeve and Aine hadn't planned a hairdo but the town was in chaos. Many of the streets were cordoned off. Defeated by the bomb hoaxers, they had decided to pamper themselves and get a free coffee and biscuit. Oonagh washed hair and watched the clock. They were still busy at five – "just as well Declan isn't here – he'd be bored rigid," she thought as she blow-dried brunette hair.

They must have changed their plans. Typical of Sean not to phone the salon. Still, she'd call him when they closed up.

She bought some fresh cream slices from the bakery on the corner – they were cheaper at closing time. Both boys loved these Saturday treats. Declan would scoff his immediately. Sean's would remain in a box in the fridge until he got in from work. As usual she bought a fruit flan for her mother – she'd pop it round on her way home.

The fruit flan was never touched. The boys – fired by thoughts of fishing had popped into the O'Callaghans on their way into town. God they were so excited – it was to be a real boy's day out. If only they hadn't stopped to natter. If only they'd left with Oonagh there would have been no soured cream cakes to bin.

A lunchtime news report from Downtown radio fired Maeve O'Callaghan's concern. The early reports of bombs and bomb hoaxes were no worry to her. They were nowhere near Oonagh and the boys. She nipped to the shops to get something nice for the tea but the pained faces of the shopkeepers indicated something was wrong. "The boys will be fine," said Paddy reassuringly – "Sure they left here long before ten, they'll have been in Bangor for hours now." He prevented her calling Oonagh at the salon – it would only worry her. "Besides – don't they listen to Downtown in there?"

"Yes. I think so," replied his wife.

They did listen to Downtown, but not on a Saturday. There was too much sport and too much news. The radio was off on Saturdays and staff members supplied cassettes of their favourite songs. They wanted Saturdays to be as special as they were for everyone else.

Declan was not with his Granny when Oonagh arrived. They called the bar – Sean must have decided to throw a sickie at least that was what Bernie the barmaid thought, "He and the wee boy are probably living it up in Bangor. Still, it's quiet enough in here so not to worry. See ya!"

It was then that Oonagh knew something was wrong. She called the hospitals, the parish priest, Sean's best friend Dermot and anyone who knew them. By ten o'clock the house was full and the last doorbell ring brought Oonagh's family life to a bitter end.

While she had fought with menopausal tresses, her boys' had fought for life. They'd gagged and choked towards silence. A concrete greyness had enveloped them in an instant, ripping them from their dreams and making them another statistic.

Maeve O'Callaghan smothered her daughter's cries and in maternal comfort, mechanically plaited a strand of tinted hair.

The funeral notices were late. Forensic issues and post mortems prolonged the grieving. Two weeks after that meaningful news bulletin Marie drove herself to the City Cemetery. She wrote letters to Oonagh, rehearsed their meeting, practised that first 'hello Oonagh, it's me' when the phone was picked up. But the letters remained unstamped, the number never dialled and the rehearsal merely a rehearsal. What she was doing was right. She would be there for her friend despite the years of silence. Typical that in her hour of need Michael was on another promotional tour – Carlos and Dino – a male singing duo from Devon of all places. Marie had inherited her mother's navigational prowess and had arrived at the church late. As befitting a woman in a mixed marriage she sat at the back. It was the usual array of off the peg suits and leather bomber jackets. Three women with very good hair sat behind Oonagh and her parents. *They must be something to do with the salon,* thought

Marie. She couldn't see Oonagh clearly but the sobbing was unmistakably hers. That quiet strong voice that had wept through 'Nobody's Child' all those years ago. Rousing words of no comfort resounded round the church. A massacre of the innocents had occurred – and yet the most innocent had been left behind to mourn.

The complementary coffins sat side by side. Scaled up or scaled down the impact was the same.

With tears in her eyes, Marie joined in the closing psalm. Her voice, unmistakable to her grieving friend, forced Oonagh to turn away from husband and child, just for an instant. The locked gaze stabbed both women – the years of loss and regret welled up. Yet there was a bittersweet comfort in the look and Marie knew she'd done the right thing.

Outside the church she looked for Oonagh but she was swapped by mourning relations so Marie waited for her parents to escort her to the graveside. Moira and James Downey had thought little of Oonagh, but they thought enough to share her grief. The drive to the cemetery took forever. Catholic women seldom stood at a graveside but Marie was part of that new breed that needed to embrace all aspects of existence.

Marie waited after interment for the main mourners to file past to offer shaken condolences. She was one of the last to embrace Oonagh – "Good to see you Marie, thank your parents for coming. Will you come back?"

"Well Oonagh I…"

"Please come back to the house, it would mean so much to Ma and Da and to me. We've missed you."

"Of course."

"Do you need a lift? Sean's brother has a spare seat."

"Och Oonagh," Marie wept, all too aware that the spare seat had been Sean's.

They walked together to the funeral car.

"Please come."

"I'll be right behind you," said Marie, closing the door of the family car.

She said goodbye to her parents and returned to the street where once they'd all been so happy.

The blinds were drawn in the small home in which the O'Dwyers lived. Two doors down, in the house that Marie had so often visited, the windows were also darkened. A ripped black flag fluttered from a lamppost – a hunger strike memorial that seemed strangely in keeping with the day. Marie parked on the corner of Bobby Sands Avenue and followed the mourners to the home that the O'Dwyers had purchased for the then newlyweds. She'd tailed a blue Ford escort from the cemetery and the occupant greeted her as warmly as the occasion permitted.

"Hello, you're Marie Downey."

"Well yes. I'm Marie Truesdale now."

"I'm Nuala, and this is my sister Susan and her husband Seamus. Eoin is our cousin. This is Marie Downey, Oonagh's best friend from school." The non-speakers nodded acknowledgement and the subdued quartet filed into the narrow hall of Oonagh's once proud home.

She sat trance-like in the darkness of the front room – surrounded by photographs of family events. Around her people whispered, eating fruitcake and drinking tea between hushed observations. Soon they'd all go and leave her to sob.

Marie approached the parker knoll chair where Oonagh sat. She knelt down beside her, clasping her hands in hers. Oonagh had seemed fine in the cemetery but had crumpled on arriving home. This was their family home and the family was no more. She looked hard at her old friend. Where had all the years gone? Why had experience put a peace wall between them? Marie held her gaze and saw in it the embarrassed eight-year-old who had weed herself. Nodding her head she felt her eyes fill with remorse. How could she have been so neglectful? With her hands cupped in remembrance Oonagh gave into her grief. She told Marie how Sean and she had met, how grand was the wedding, and how joyous was her son's birth. She rummaged around for photographs, occasionally smiling between tears.

The mourners filtered away and soon only Marie and the O'Callaghans were left. Oonagh was exhausted. "Best have a wee lie down love." Padraig O'Callaghan and his wife looked old. Marie helped Oonagh up the stairs and said goodbye. "Give her a wee call tomorrow – if you can – here's the number."

"I will Mrs O'Callaghan, I promise." Holding the crumpled paper in her hand Marie walked back to the car. She too was exhausted but couldn't sleep. Her past life was at odds with her present. There was too much in the remembering. Oonagh and she had years to cover.

Chapter Eight

A tenth anniversary is usually cause for celebration but to Marie Truesdale (nee Downey) it was merely a cause for concern. Each day Michael swelled the guest list by adding yet more clients and contacts. He seldom used the F word – friendship was not of great importance to him. Brokering deals was Michael's thing and a 'little soiree', as he called it, was too good an opportunity to be wasted. The phone in the downstairs office ran constantly that week and by Wednesday Marie was all too aware that her intimate dinner party had become a performing circus with many of the acts under-rehearsed. Oonagh was a godsend. She acted as a sponge for Marie's angst and was only too pleased to feel of affectionate use. While waiting for the NIO to compensate her – how could you compensate anyone for the loss of a perfect future, total destruction and the abandonment of hope she had started to fall apart. Mrs O'Callaghan and Marie were on the phone constantly. Neither knew what to do and their conversations, overheard by Oonagh, made her situation worse. Returning to Anne's was just too painful. She tried but with each gesture of sympathy, each time she saw the clock and looked towards the door expectantly her eyes would fill with tears of injustice and one of the other girls would have to finish off her client. Nuala didn't know how to deal with Oonagh's grief – she was still coming to terms with her own. Seeking refuge in the Parker-knoll chair of memory Oonagh retreated from the salon and the world. One April morning, Marie awoke and knew exactly what to do.

"Morning, Oonagh. Get dressed. I need your help." The shock of seeing Marie on her doorstep at eight o'clock in the morning and the business-like manner in which the plea issued forced Oonagh to obey. "Oh and bring a photo of the boys." The photo was given pride of place in Marie's front room and Oonagh was given little jobs to keep her mind off the subject. She did Marie's hair every Friday, helped her with the shopping, dusted her cherished photograph and all Marie's expensive possessions and, before she was aware of it, began a new routine. Initially, she wouldn't accept payment but Marie's constant attempts to hand over Truesdale cash finally wore her down. Together they would venture out to the Lisburn Road, discovering the odd misplaced exotic shop and purchasing girly necessities. A new nail polish gave endless possibilities for chat and, gradually, with each outing their buried friendship was exhumed. Marie always made sure the cash was wrapped in a thank you card – a way of apologising for her twelve-year absence.

The tenth anniversary supper dominated a whole week and Oonagh became Marie's second in command. Michael Truesdale – "Oh just a few drinks and a wee bite" – had no idea what the girls were planning but knew his wife wouldn't let him down. Sure, she was a naïve schoolgirl when he met her but he'd groomed her to be the perfect partner. She'd make sure everyone would see how well he was doing and he'd left some signed cheques to cover the necessities. Essential to all such dos was the appearance of the hostess and over a morning coffee and a shortbread finger Oonagh was persuaded to accompany Marie to Renee Meneeley's. She'd never been inside this style emporium. While waiting for a bus at the City Hall, she'd stared at its windows, wondering who had the money to shop there: now she knew. They took a bus into town but got off just before Ormeau Avenue. Marie said the little walk would do them good but Oonagh knew that it was just in case anyone in the posh shop saw them arrive on public transport. Her 'of course' response made Marie laugh; Oonagh knew her far too well. They were giggling girls when they pushed through the doors of Escada heaven. A tinkling bell summoned the sales lieutenant. She was an elegant woman in her fifties, hair swept into an evening chignon fastened with a tortoiseshell clip. Painted lips and painted nails were the only highlight in her grey palette. Walking towards customer or time waster she exuded a cold confidence developed during lunchtime fashion parades in the Orpheus Rooms. She'd been all set for catwalk stardom, everyone in Cherry valley said so, but a cloudy marriage and a thundery divorce had darkened her skies so here she was; a too old shop girl selling clothes to those too young to have any style. "Good morning ladies, may we help you?" With an insincere, "I do hope so," Marie told of her grand soiree and Pandora (real name Betty) paraded chiffon, silk, taffeta and fine wool for approval. Oonagh sat on a chair designed for older occupants and watched her friend glide effortlessly and repeatedly in and out of the changing room. Initially Oonagh was flustered on being asked to comment but by outfit three she felt confident enough to speak her mind. Pandora thought everything beautiful – she would, she was on commission.

They settled on a black satin cocktail dress with a ribboned front and chiffon sleeves. Marie had the perfect marquisate brooch to compliment it. "And for my friend." Oonagh looked shocked as she was ushered into a changing room. "Marie, I..." she whispered. "Look, it's all coming out of the business. Sod it. I owe you so much Oonagh O'Callaghan so shut up and try this on."

They settled on a brown crepe dress with a chiffon overlay. It was beautiful. "I've got some jade earrings you can borrow that will look great on you – oh, separate bags please." Leaving Pandora to tidy up the two ladies walked their Renee Meneeley carrier bags through the security barriers to Sawers. Marie had prepared a list of items to be delivered on Friday morning – "On account please."

"Certainly, Mrs Truesdale." Marie never seemed to hand over cash for anything. This worried Oonagh. How could she keep a handle on her housekeeping? The truth was Marie didn't and it didn't matter. Business was booming and the money was there to be spent. "Just a couple more things to get and then a wee spot of lunch I think." Marie was on a roll and Oonagh knew better than to reason with her. The dismissal of the Bally shoe shop as being 'far too old' gave Oonagh a clue as to what the couple of more things were. Two Roland Cartier bags added to their spoils. Oonagh had insisted on buying her own brown suede sling backs, Marie had given in but had insisted on purchasing green and brown shoe bows because they would complement the earrings. "Besides, you'll probably be wearing your hair up to give you a bit more height and I've got a green-ribboned slide that'll tie it all in." Where style was concerned there was no faulting Marie – she was her mother's daughter. Two open sandwiches and two frothy coffees at the Skandia allowed the girls, time to dissect their purchases and the other tables in the restaurant. Oonagh felt guilty. She still had the upstairs to finish and it was nearly two. This was the first of many plans to go awry that week.

Michael was office-bound the day before the party. This was not through choice – Marie had put her foot down – how could she be expected to answer the 'bloody phones' and to take bookings when there was 'all this to be done'. With such a strident tone in the observation Michael thought it best to comply and had locked himself in the downstairs office. Oonagh was collected at seven thirty, not a problem for her as these days she slept little. Recurring re-enactments of that fateful Saturday curtailed her slumber; a cup of tea and a rich tea biscuit her only solace. For the first few months after the funeral she'd gobbled fig rolls but these had started to disagree with her. It was her mother who had recommended the alternative for she too was a light sleeper. Marie talked all the way to the Malone Road. A mixture of annoyance, excitement, optimism and panic infused every sentence. Oonagh grunted agreement to everything – Marie was always happier that way. By eight forty five the kitchen was littered with boxes. Downing a quick Gold Blend for instant sophistication they set about restoring order. Michael still hadn't finished the guest list despite Marie's constant nagging and so Marie 'just to be on the safe side' had decided to work on a plus ten basis. Today was puddings, tomorrow, savouries, flowers and finishing touches. Her mother had organised the cake and mushroom patties as a gift so that was something. The next-door neighbours, the O'Keefes had offered spare fridge capacity and Moya O'Keefe had insisted on making three of her fattening but scrumptious strawberry cheesecakes. She had a small cottage industry making puddings for people who passed them off as their own. As her business expanded the fraud was exposed – no one could make a cheesecake like Moya. Marie had also ordered two chocolate meringue roulades as a standby. While Oonagh pressed tablecloths for breakfast room, lounge and dining room, Marie re-arranged her lists, checked her recipes with the Galloping Gourmet and placed ingredients in battle lines. Cooking was a challenge for Marie; her dishes always delightfully garnished, seldom lived up to their appearances. She had a heavy hand with pastry and spices. While she fretted over where to start Oonagh simply got on with things. Marriage to Michael had eroded much of Marie's self-belief – sure she could put on a show in public, she could rise to the challenge but after the first few years, they were seldom together in public and her husband rarely challenged her positively. She was always fitting in with his plans. Consequently she did everything for his approval and he seldom noticed her efforts.

While she dunked ginger biscuits in sweet sherry and sandwiched them together with whipped cream, Lynda-Jane blasted out sun-filled dedications. Marie liked listening to the radio. It kept her in touch with things. Sean Rafferty and Wendy Austin woke her on radio Ulster. Lynda-Jane and Big T got her through the afternoon. With Oonagh in the kitchen she worried about the news bulletins. Oddly enough Oonagh found the half-hourly musical stabs a comfort. It was good to know she was not alone, that other women were experiencing her experiences; perhaps grief could unite people after all.

Marie thought her ginger log's a triumph. Oonagh thought them a little homemade looking but kept her own counsel. This was Marie's special party pudding, she'd seen her make it dozens of times but Oonagh still couldn't see what all the fuss was about. It always tasted fine but it was just some ginger nuts, cream and sherry. Where was the skill in that? For Marie, it was brilliance by association. Her drama teacher had produced it with aplomb during a dinner party given for her and Michael when they returned from Portstewart. Mrs Watt had confided the recipe to Marie and naturally she felt obliged to continue this artistic tradition. It wasn't the only culinary delight she'd inherited. A red onion and tomato salad, a spaghetti dish topped with crushed crisps and homemade brawn also displayed her cultural heritage. Oonagh had sampled all of these dishes in the past year and they were not a patch on her mother's stew or Nuala's chopped ham, carrot and onion pie. Oonagh kept these culinary secrets locked safely in her own kitchen.

As Marie fretted over which shelf was best for cooling her creations Oonagh got on with the chocolate mousse and apple strudel. She had intended to make a black forest gateau but Marie said that everyone was doing that now. By lunchtime the kitchen was a war zone. There was no sign of lunch so Michael took himself off to the golf club 'for a chicken Maryland' and doubtless a few vodka lime and sodas.

By three o'clock the pudding queens had completed their reign. Its worth would be judged the following evening and probably be deemed inferior to that of the next-door princess but, for the moment, both Marie and Oonagh were content. They sat among the spoils sipping Bacardi and coke – "God, there's stacks to do, you'll just have to stay over. I'll drive you home after this and you can get a few things gathered together." Oonagh was doubly worried; firstly because Marie was necking the alcohol, she always did so when she felt under pressure, and secondly because since the bombing she'd not spent a single night out of Sean's bed. "You could pick me up in the morning."

"Nonsense," replied Marie. "God knows what time the deliveries will arrive and we could do the flowers and tables this evening to get ahead. Besides, you'll have to do my hair in the morning – there's no way I'm greeting the agency freaks looking like one of them." With a light giggle Oonagh gave in.

Since their reunion she'd wondered what kind of relationship Michael and Marie had. On the surface it all seemed lovey-dovey enough but she sensed little real warmth – perhaps that's what happens to childless couples. She'd asked Marie if they had ever thought of having a family. Once, only once had she asked. The answer had surprised her and warned her off the subject. Michael, it seemed, didn't want children. His business was his family. The Marie she knew obviously did but had given up the idea early on. Oonagh sensed an emptiness in their relationship. It lacked heart. When they talked of their childhood with all its failings, it was then and only then that Marie seemed truly alive. Wealth had killed something within her and Oonagh couldn't understand why. Michael arrived in as they were leaving, "Oonagh's staying over for a couple of days."

"Great," smiled Michael clearly thinking the opposite. "At least that way I'll have someone to talk to other than my parents."

"Oh shit, are they coming?"

"No show without mother." Michael wished Marie's mother a permanent no-show. Oonagh was looking forward to seeing them again. It had been a long time after all.

71

Oonagh collected her new things, still in their new bags, grabbed a few toiletries and Declan's football shirt and jumped back into Marie's car. She could never be far away from her boys. They swung by a Lisburn Road florist. There was no plan to their purchases. Marie would mix some flowers with 'stuff' from the garden. Oonagh advised the purchase of some oasis and florist wire. She'd seen her mother do altarpieces for the church and knew these items were essential, somehow. The florist offered to make them a centrepiece to copy there and then. Keeping one eye on the car and another on him they marvelled first at his speed and then at his generosity as he threw it in for nothing. He belonged to Michael's golf club and probably needed a return favour sometime very soon. Fragrant non-denominational flowers perfumed Marie's Volkswagen run-around. Her driving reflected the vehicle – low mileage and high expectation. Fortunately, erratic parking in your own driveway was always permitted.

They unloaded the plants and set to. Copying the set piece was unsettling. Although they had paid attention in the shop their efforts that began too large ended up looking stunted. Dwarfed in large bowls or overflowing in small vases their floral efforts left them in disarray and they needed more Bacardi and coke for their nerves. They should have just followed their instincts but life had made these untrustworthy. After two large ones they ventured into the garden, armed with kitchen scissors and revengeful abandonment. The resulting floral arrangements were decadent, free form and a little bohemian – if these flowers said anything it was likely to be, "if you don't like it, fuck off."

"Do you think Miss Slevin ever got married?"

"No," replied Oonagh, "I suspect she'll always live in Rome."

"You don't mean she's become a nun?"

"God no, she's probably teaching English to the children of an Italian Count."

"And goes to Mass, every day." In tune they laughed and proclaimed, "Poor Mr Teakle."

This opened the door to a room of childhood remembrances. They abandoned the burnt frozen pizza. They abandoned food altogether. They abandoned themselves to a shared past.

Chapter Nine

The six a.m. alarm was not welcomed by Marie. Last night's antics had taken their toll and a Bacardi head was her first morning sensation. The second, the unpleasant dampness of Michael's hairy back. She hadn't heard him get in yet here he was, snoring like a piglet unaware of its breakfast future. Gingerly she rolled back the covers and rose to greet the day. Fuck there was a lot to do – thank God Oonagh was there to help. She showered in the en-suite not daring to look in the mirror and went downstairs to the breakfast room. Oonagh was already seated at the table waiting for company. She'd been there most of the night just waiting. The room she'd been put in was fine, some would say 'fab', but trendiness never impressed Oonagh. She always liked to know just where she stood. It was fine, the room, but like her own bedroom it was empty and at four o'clock she'd risen, washed and come downstairs for company. "How's your head, want an Alka-Seltzer?"

"No thanks Marie, I'm fine, all set to crack on. Happy Anniversary."

Oonagh handed over a small bag. "It's not very much…"

"Oh Oonagh, it's lovely." Ever the impatient one, Marie had untied the pale green ribbon from the box and revealed its contents; an oval picture frame with a picture from the past – a photo of two wee girls at the Pierrots. "I noticed you didn't have many photos of yourself and this one's always been a bit special for me." Marie was touched by the gift. Where were those girls now? She kissed her friend, put some coffee in the coffee filter and went into the drawing room to find a new home for this childhood memory. "Oonagh, come here. What do you think?" To Oonagh's delight Marie had placed her gift on the mantelpiece, where Sean and Declan's picture resided. "Shit – I've got to wrap Michael's present." Rushing to the cupboard under the stairs, her secret hiding place, Marie produced a sheet of wrapping paper and a bag from Lunns. "I bought him these, what do you think?" Lunns was Belfast's top jewellers so it was no surprise to Oonagh that the silk-lined box contained something lovely. Marie had chosen well. The gold cufflinks with the diamond corner were just right for Michael – chunky and a bit flash. She'd have preferred to buy him a new watch but he wouldn't part with the old Omega he'd been wearing when they first met. She'd considered a tiepin but they were too fiddly and Michael would get more wear from these gold trinkets. "Mind if I use your ribbon?"

"Not at all." Oonagh did indeed mind. She'd chosen the ribbon because it was Marie's favourite childhood colour. Her mother had made several summer dresses in just that shade. Such pale green fineness would never be appreciated by the likes of Michael Truesdale. "Your present, darling. Happy Anniversary. Morning, Oonagh." Michael kissed his wife and handed over a Lunns gift bag. *How well they know each other,* thought Oonagh. "Happy Anniversary – Oh my God, they're lovely." The ivy shaped Marquisite and pearl earrings were indeed lovely. In fact they matched the brooch she'd received on their last anniversary. "Here's a little something for my favourite husband." Oonagh felt a little uncomfortable, as if she'd caught a friend naked in the bathroom. Almost dismissing his gift with 'they're lovely dear' Michael Truesdale poured himself some coffee, announced he'd be out of town for most of the day and as on most mornings had a hot then cold shower. "A bacon sandwich to keep us going?"

Thank God, thought Oonagh whose stomach was beginning to think her throat was cut. "Aye, that'll be lovely and then we'll make a start on your hair." The Denny's rashers were lovely, not too salty and with Golden Cow butter and Mother's Pride bread the girls had a feast worthy of their day of army manoeuvres. Dishes speedily done, they climbed to Marie's bedroom and Oonagh began the shampooing, roller-ing and combing that would transform day into evening. She wrapped her fine creation in a silk scarf and while Marie made a few calls and mangled a few Benson & Hedges, she did her own hair in a slightly less grand manner.

A ten o'clock doorbell summoned both chignoned friends downstairs. It was the lad from Sawers with a delivery for 'Mrs Tuesday'. Too busy laughing to correct him, Marie and Oonagh helped him unload box after box. The Ormeau bread van delivered soon after but Marie just took her normal consignment. Penny, from two doors down, had promised to collect a dozen baguettes from the new French Boulangerie on the Dublin Road – that would certainly show the neighbourhood who was boss. Delighted that their floral creations had survived the night, Marie and Oonagh began to climb the mountain that was 'entertaining at home'.

A salmon dressed, a chicken crowned and a beef bourguignoned all by one o'clock. By three, the buffet tables began to groan with rice salads, bean salads, potato salads and salad salads. Pride of place was a clove ham and a rare roast beef – both waiting to be unwrapped since the ten o'clock delivery. It was then that finesse set in and teamwork became paramount. They wrapped breadsticks in streaky bacon – one hour of activity giving only seconds of pleasure. These were always wolfed down as soon as they appeared on the buffet. They filled salami saucers with curried egg and made boats out of celery. A fruit cup was made at six, a celebration punch at six thirty and with glasses and silver plate polished by seven the girls had one hour to get ready.

Oonagh combed out Marie's hair and helped her to dress. She looked beautiful. Annoyingly, Marie was still finishing her make-up and putting on her new earrings when the doorbell rang. The continual pressing was aggressive – *It can only be my mother,* thought Marie. Shoes in hand she ran downstairs and greeted the Downey trio clutching boxes from Bells. Naturally, Oonagh heard the kafuffle but was too busy enjoying the 'Renee Meneeley experience' to give it much of her attention. The dress glided over her body, its silky coolness made her feel special – "If only Sean were here to zip me up." She smiled a watery-eyed smile in the full-length mirror, climbed up into her shoes and turned to see a flustered Marie in the doorway. "Trust my mother to get here early. I'm sure she's just checking that things are to her satisfaction. You look brill. Oh, here are the earrings and don't forget the shoe bows. When you are ready, be a doll and make sure my family doesn't eat us out of house and home before the guests arrive." Oonagh laughed, completed her look and, once it was all 'tied in', went down to greet the Downeys. *Holy Mary, Mother of God,* thought Moira Downey, turning to see Oonagh. "Her compensation must have come through already." She stopped plating vol au vents and stretched out her arms to greet Oonagh. "Don't you look a picture? What a beautiful dress. What lovely shoes, oh and those earrings…"

"Well, it's all…"

"Who would guess you'd not long lost your family?" Oonagh was taken aback. She didn't know what to say. Sure, Moira Downey had always looked down on her but she'd never thought her nasty before now. She had barely recovered when James Downey threw his arms round her. "Well, would you look at you? Doesn't Oonagh look bloody marvellous Niall?" The spotty adolescent blushed. "He's not normally that shy," piped up Moira Downey, oblivious to her previous faux pas. "You should have seen him play Bardolph this year in the school production. Mr Grime was very pleased."

Bardolph spoke, "Is there any food?"

"Yes Niall, lots but Marie wants to uncover it later – punch anyone?"

Oonagh guided her once lost second family into the drawing room and distributed one fruit cup and two glasses of punch. It seemed like ages before Marie arrived but only to Oonagh. Marie seemed annoyed when she came down the stairs and Oonagh didn't know why. Checking her make-up in the landing mirror Marie had overheard her mother's unkindness. How had her father put up with that all these years? "Don't we look a grand pair?" said Marie, putting her arm around Oonagh's waist. "I wouldn't be anywhere without my best friend." *Now that should silence the cow for a while at least,* she thought.

They were unwrapping the platters when Michael arrived – "Sorry, sorry, I'll just jump in the shower." Marie and Oonagh downed a second glass of punch and waited for the real guests to arrive. A pudding'd up Moya O'Keefe and her husband took over the kitchen followed swiftly by the baguette-brandishing neighbours. Michael did most of the introductions and the drink ladling and soon a party atmosphere descended. It wasn't long before Squire Truesdale had unlocked the drinks cabinet, demanded more ice and begun to concoct cocktails for his coterie. Oonagh had never seen such a collection of opinionated individuals, their strange variety matching the drinks Michael made. Moira Downey was in her element. She was an 'artiste' and these were her kind of people. Only Marie knew how deluded she was. Her mother had decided to dress for the occasion; quite what she thought the occasion to be was hardly reflected in the green and lemon swirling sleeves of a polyester hostess gown. Actually, it was probably silk but the whole effect, like its owner, was synthetic.

"Troy, how do you know my lovely daughter and son-in-law?" It was amusing first to Marie and then Oonagh that Moira Downey had alighted on Northern Ireland's first male stripper. "Well actually Mrs err…"

"Call me Moira."

"I work for them."

"How marvellous," twittered the now giddy mother of the hostess. "And what exactly do you do? What is your act?" Troy hesitated. "No, no don't tell me, let me guess." Her ridiculous and futile attempts only made things worse. So Marie eventually put Troy out of his misery, "Troy's a stripper mother, ten inches of pleasure – isn't that right Troy?"

"Absolutely – lovely to speak with you Moira, great party Marie, thanks." Mrs Downey whimpered in disgust. Marie returned the look – that would teach her mother to not poke her nose in everywhere. Ten inches of pleasure was just what Moira Downey needed.

Marie went to find Troy to top up his glass and to see that he was alright. Of all their clients she liked him best. He was honest about his talent, honest about what he did with it, never cancelled a gig and was always on time. Most of the others, unless Michael and she held their hands, could barely wipe their own arses. Perhaps Eric from Pazazz could be forgiven – he was blind and Suzy his keyboard player probably needed to develop all her talents. The rest just wanted a wet nurse and the childless Marie had outgrown that function long ago.

Dawn Chorus stood at the bookcase sipping a Singapore Sling. Dawn, real name Richard Singer, was popular on the cabaret circuit, particularly with businessmen. They knew they were buggering a bloke but convinced themselves that Richard was really a woman at heart. Off duty he'd dress up for them and join in the deception. Ulster women loved the risqué nature of his act. He could say things to men that no Ulster woman could. Dawn Chorus could get away with murder but tonight was not hers and so Richard, in full slap, loitered by the bookcase hoping to solicit a golf club member. Several of those were in attendance, Alan, Owen and Gerry to be precise but they were much more interested in the antics of 'the amazing Keith' to tee off with a man in woman's clothing. 'The Amazing Keith' was not the only person to parade his act. It was easy for him; being a close up magician not many people noticed. He spent much of the evening with Niall Downey until the Holywood am-dram queen spotted the goings-on and, goaded by three 'Black Russians', decided to put an end to it. Keira Fitzsimmons, that year's disco dancing champion and a new signing for the agency would be better company for her son. She could bring him out of himself. She too, however, had a mother in attendance and the two embarrassed teenagers wished themselves dead on meeting.

Three quarters of the Fab Four, the lead singer absent due to a 'thick throat' helped Marie serve the hot food and arrange the desserts. 'She Bang' the all-girl group from Ballina had double helpings. Starved by their father, their former manager, they made up for days of abstinence by troughing when he wasn't around. Their costumes gaped on stage but they didn't care – "Sure, what's wrong with a bit of flesh these days?" Marie could never remember who was who so a general, "How you doing girls?" was all she ever said to them. Neither Oonagh nor Marie had seen girls of their age eat so freely and Moira Downey's labelling it 'a disgrace' encouraged Marie to offer them more helpings of ginger log. It had been slow to leave the dessert table but now with She Bang's help Marie would not be put to shame by her neighbour's offerings. So busy was she with desserts that she hadn't noticed Michael slip into the office to take a call. As they cut into the Bell's cake he whispered, "I've got to pop out for half an hour on business. Hold the fort love; you're doing a great job." He slipped away after his short speech. The woman who had made him so happy was pissed off. Here, she had to cover up for him again. As the singing began, her mother and the other acts all trying to outdo each other, she, along with Oonagh and her father sought refuge in the kitchen comforting each other with stories of the past and large vodka tonics. Marie was pleased to see her father so relaxed. It wasn't easy being married to a demanding jaded chorus girl whose talents were strictly amateur. Her mother kept a lovely home and had made sure the children were well turned out but it was always for someone else's benefit – they were always on show.

James hadn't seen his daughter's friend since the funeral. Then they had had no time to talk but now with a potent 'Och Oonagh' and safe from the prying judgement of his wife he encouraged his daughter's friend to share her grief and fill a void with pride. "You are not doing too bad, all things considered and if I can ever be of any help please give me a ring. You're worth ten of those bloody hangers on."

"Now Dad…" admonished Marie. "Oh I know, I was only saying."

"Another refill Mr Downey?" enquired Oonagh rescuing both her friends.

Troy was the first to leave. He'd grown tired of the singing and of people asking him if Troy was his real name. Did they really think Aughnacloy farmers were that imaginative and shouldn't these luvvies know better anyway? He had a gig at eleven and, perfectly mannered as always, had sought out his hosts to convey his gratitude. "Oh, wait 'til Michael gets back. He said he wouldn't be long."

"Sorry Marie, I've got our money to earn. Oh, I'm dropping Richard off at Parliament – he's meeting some bloke from Hillsborough."

"Well, tell him to be careful. You know what those government types are like and tell him not to make a weekend of it. He's got a full week of bookings next week."

"Sure. I'll tell him and thanks again."

"Not a bad bloke considering what he does for a living," chuckled James Downey. "Och Dad, you've been living with that wife of yours for far too long."

Worried that she'd be accused of neglecting her guests Marie wandered back into the lounge and through the drawing room. She needn't have been concerned. There were too many egos screaming for attention for anyone to notice her. For a while she stood at the partition archway – the contemporary divide that fused both rooms and gazed at the mayhem. *Where the fuck is Michael?* she thought. *These are his bloody friends.* She stood aside as Keira Fitzsimmons pushed her little brother towards the downstairs toilet – perhaps he was more advanced than she thought. The sound of retching reassured her. Obviously Niall had not been drinking fruit cup all evening and Keira would remain a virgin. Oonagh handed the disco diva a glass of tap water for Niall and returned to the kitchen for another vodka.

"I'd best be going love; it's time to get your mother home before she runs off with the circus. Tell that husband of yours it's been a great night. He'll never know what he's missed." It wasn't easy to drag Moira away. She was about to launch into 'Fernando' for the second time, her songs from "Oliver!" not having gone as well as she'd expected. Fortunately Niall's 'sudden illness' gave James the excuse he needed and Moira a new dramatic role. Marie showed her parents to the door, angry that Michael had let her down in front of her mother yet again. Oonagh had waved them off from the bottom of the stairs and saw Marie's disappointment; "Fuck him," bit Marie, "Let's have another drink." They filled new glasses in the drawing room and before a second mouthful Marie was on her feet venting her anger on 'Four Green Fields'. As she sang her annoyance left her. She began to remember just how much she enjoyed an audience, how much she loved singing. By the time she'd conquered 'Three Cigarettes in an Ashtray' – that Patsy Cline love classic, Marie was in her element. Michael who had encouraged her singing in the early days wasn't even there to share the applause. She'd have liked to sing a song especially for him but instead she finished her set with 'But not for me'.

A sharp knock on the front door cut through the jollity. It was late for revellers and seldom did Marie answer the door after ten thirty. The judge's wife three doors down had made that mistake; her RUC protection officer had failed to protect. The knocking like on that occasion was persistent and Marie and Oonagh fired with alcohol and a party atmosphere went into the hall. Instinctively the partygoers quietened. Marie and Oonagh cautiously approached the inner glass door; the shadow of a small man was clearly visible. With a sharp intake of breath Marie threw back the front door. "I'm here for the girls," a dirty white minibus spluttered in the drive. "Tell 'em to get a move on. I've another job at two." There was no need to ask which girls. The family resemblance was all too obvious and laughing nervously Marie and Oonagh watched as the five now larger members of 'She Bang' clambered into Uncle Seamus' much-abused vehicle. On closing the door Marie and Oonagh's laughter was externalised. How had they been so frightened by such a wee man with such a shit van? They returned to the guests and after another half hour surveyed the damage alone. "Well, I think they enjoyed themselves – don't you?"

"They ate and drank enough anyway," said Oonagh emptying party remains into black bin bags that were normally kept for garden waste. "What shall we do with the empty bottles?"

"Oh," replied Marie somewhat shocked by the variety and number, "We'll box them up for the dump in the morning. Bollocks to this. I can't be arsed. We'll do it all tomorrow. Michael might be back in time to give us a hand. Fancy a wee nightcap?" The two old and rediscovering friends sat among the remnants of the party sipping vodka and flat tonic.

Oonagh wondered what Michael was playing at. Was there another woman? Had he fallen in with a dodgy crowd? But the fact that Marie was nonplussed convinced her that perhaps this was a regular occurrence. With a 'goodnight, God bless' they closed their separate bedroom doors and awaited the arrival of guilt-ridden hangovers.

Marie slept badly that evening. She dreamt of a gig where she forgot her act, where no one applauded and there was no sign of Michael offering support. At three thirty she awoke, her nightdress dampened by anxiety and turned to Michael for reassurance – he still wasn't there. Was this the start of another three-day bender? According to Michael, it was all part of the business. Over the years she had grown to accept it. He was always very attentive when he returned but to start on the night of their anniversary, now that was something else. She wondered what Oonagh must have thought, Oonagh who almost every night awoke to mourn an absence in her bed. At least Michael always returned.

Marie went down to the kitchen and, without looking at the party evidence, cut herself a slab of cheesecake and poured a tumbler of milk. Sweet things consoled her when Michael was away. As she scraped the dairy produce off her fork she thought about the evening. She enjoyed the singing most of all – even if the audience had been sycophantic. Keeping the office and the house going was fine but it didn't give her the buzz of standing on stage doing her bit. Perhaps she'd try to broker the subject with Michael once again. He didn't think it a suitable occupation for his wife and that was that. It wasn't safe out there for her. Yet he was prepared to risk everyone else, all those who had crowded round her buffet table and guzzled her drinks. Aware of a sore head as she finished her cheesecake Marie downed two paracetamol with a final mouthful of milk and went back to bed.

The hangovers came as hangovers do. Oonagh had been up three times during the night; twice with phantom vomiting and once to regurgitate a full party buffet supper. She'd sluiced her mouth with tap water, fearful of going down to the kitchen for a glass and had pressed a cold damp flannel to her head as she clutched the toilet bowl. What would Sean say if he ever saw her like this? Looking down on her now he was either laughing or crying. With such guilt the pounding in her head worsened. There were very few drinkers in her family. Most of them liked a few jars but it was only her uncle Eoin who had developed a real taste for the stuff. He'd been out of touch for years, working on the roads, or so they said but his yellow waxen face shining out of a slim coffin had stayed with her. Although only eight she'd been made to kiss him goodbye in the front parlour of Granny Tully's. Her Da never touched a drop since but perhaps the disease had skipped a generation and she was its next victim. That was it. She would never touch a drop of the stuff again. Besides, there was Sean and Declan to think of.

For both women the three flights of stairs to the hallway were a challenge that morning. They barely spoke over tea and plain toast and when they did it was only to mutter, "Oh God, I feel awful." Even the thud of the day's post falling on the tiled porch was a trauma. After their second pot of tea accompanied by a mutual, "That's it, I'm never drinking again," Marie remembered the almost out of date Alka-Seltzer in the bathroom cabinet. Oonagh hadn't had Alka-Seltzer since her pregnancy. She didn't take it because she thought herself pregnant – for three months her upset stomach had become a stomach ulcer. It was only when Dr Casement had given them the good news that she had stopped taking it. The white fizziness reminded her of her lost boy and the potion, designed to settle her stomach, unsettled her.

Mechanically the two friends started the slow clear-up process. There was a sadness about it all. Platefuls of desire had become symbols of rejection, the flowers had drooped and candle wax and fag ash soiled the once crisp linen. By lunchtime the smell of stale smoke and flat beer had been replaced by spring pledge and L'air du temps. Even the carpet bar one ginger cigarette burn looked fresh. Marie decided to do sausages and chips for lunch. She made enough for Michael but he didn't show. Oonagh took the bus home, her Renee Meneeley bag clutched tightly to her and a doggy bag on her lap.

Chapter Ten

After mass on Sunday, she always went to the ten o'clock, Oonagh called Marie. She always did so on a Sunday – partly to organise her week but mainly to check on her friend. "Will you come round for lunch? I don't want to be on my own." Oonagh knew that Michael hadn't been in touch and sensed worry in her friend's voice. Her parents would understand. Since the bomb they had taken it in turn about to visit for lunch – it was her parents' turn this week – she'd pop in and explain before Marie collected her. It was unlike Marie to be late – Michael had taught her well. She'd have done the Supermac run earlier in the week; Michael always liked a nice roast dinner on a Sunday when he was home. There was no chance of last minute shopping on Sunday in Belfast and Garages weren't really Marie's thing. "Sorry I'm late, one of the bloody acts has phoned in sick and I've been trying to find a replacement. You might have to give me a hand with the dinner." While Oonagh prepared the vegetables, tended to the beef and made what she hoped was the batter for the Yorkshire pudding, Marie bashed the wall phone in the kitchen. She was still joyless as they sat down to lunch. "Bloody typical, Michael away and that cow Donna gets a throat infection – I didn't know you could get that by lying on your back."

"Now Marie," laughed Oonagh, gently reprimanding her friend. "Normally it wouldn't matter but this is a big GAA gig – good money, new venue, who knows where it could lead?"

"Have they seen her before?" enquired Oonagh. "Only a black and white picture – Michael never invests in a colour print unless it's an established artiste."

"What's her act?"

"Oh the usual standards – the type of stuff I used to do." Oonagh had an idea.

"What time does it start?"

"Oh, at about nine o'clock."

"Well, why don't you do it?" Marie initially laughed at the suggestion but as she polished off the last of the roast beef and her third glass of red wine it seemed like a good solution. "We've got three hours to do the transformation – get me a picture of her." Oonagh cleared away the Sunday lunch and put on her cleaning overall. Marie phoned the venue and the house band, went over her set and within an hour had agreed to become Donna. She had no idea what had made her say yes but once she had confirmed Donna's appearance at 'The Limelight' and talked with the keyboard player she could hardly back down. Oonagh's driving was likely to be the most dangerous aspect of the performance but they'd just have to cope. Marie had only ever talked to Donna on the phone. She was one of Michael's protégés and so they only had her filed publicity shot to go on. From her own knowledge of what Michael liked (Oh my God, what would he say) Marie guessed at what Donna would wear and chose a long black skirt and a sequinned Frank Usher top, low cut, it was exactly what Michael would have chosen – in fact, he'd chosen this very top for Marie's final gig. She'd thought about trousers but the GAA was quite traditional and so had gone against that Donna-lead idea.

Ushered into the shower by Oonagh, who was preparing her 'workstation' at the dressing table, Marie was sick with worry. What if Michael came home now? How could she explain this moment of madness? Of course, he'd blame Oonagh – "You're as thick as thieves you two"– but none of this was Oonagh's fault. It was a sensible business decision and for that he would only have himself to blame. After all, how often had he said, "The show must go on." Marie was merely following his dictum. Deep down Marie knew she was guilty of much more than that. She was making a stand, escaping, for one night only, the shackles of marriage and doing something she really loved. As she applauded her decision, wrapped in a towelling dressing gown, the magnitude of what she was about to do struck her – what if someone recognised her – what if they refused to pay cash as agreed? What if Donna ever heard about it? ~If the walk to the dressing table had been any longer, she would have changed her mind but seeing Oonagh so charged, so keen to make a go of it, she hadn't the heart to turn back.

"Right," said Oonagh, clutching the photograph, "more tarty I think." Marie's hair was a similar length to Donna's but it lacked the height evident in the picture. Deftly Oonagh went to work with heated rollers and a tail comb. With copious amounts of lacquer and minutes of elbow tiring backcombing, she soon achieved a passable similarity. Once Marie had applied her usual foundation Oonagh chiselled out cheekbones, lips and eyelids. The look was still Marie but with an overlay of Dame Donna Showbiz. Thank God the Frank Usher top buttoned up the back or Marie would have had to perform in her slip.

The undercover agent and her best friend set off just after four. They needed to give themselves plenty of time to navigate Newry, locate the venue and meet the boys from the band. It was an awards supper dance so Marie would just have to pray the sound was okay – only locals could afford to pop in for a sound check. Tonight Marie would be performing with 'The Newry Beats' so they'd probably been sound checking since lunchtime.

As Oonagh ground the gears along Derryvolgie Avenue, Marie unfolded the road map and tightly gripped the scrap of paper bearing directions to the venue. They hardly spoke to each other along the way – each aware of the importance of what they were doing. Oonagh had never had to concentrate so hard on anything. She was fearful of driving such a long distance, frightened of stumbling on a UDR checkpoint and concerned that her friend would urge her, at any moment to turn back. Marie had never lied so convincingly before. She'd never betrayed her husband and in fact she was quite enjoying it. As the car steamed up they opened and closed windows to alleviate stress and avoid make-up run. They found 'The Limelight' easily and in good time; who the hell could miss a bright yellow building on the approach to Newry town centre. The car park was filling up. The 'do' started at seven thirty but Donna wasn't on till nine, after the prize giving and the dinner. Marie didn't want to go in so early in case someone recognised her but Oonagh thought it odd for two women to be sitting so long in the car park and so they tottered over the gravel to a side entrance near the kitchen. "Hello. I'm Donna and this is my manager Marie Truesdale, I think you were speaking to her earlier today." Suddenly Oonagh was forced to become Marie. "Indeed I was. It's always a pleasure doing business with Truesdale talent. The bands are just inside waiting for you. Eamonn the keyboard player can't wait to meet you. You go on in and I'll settle up here with your boss." Oonagh realised that meant her. "So how is Michael? Jesus I haven't seen him for ages." Oonagh regaled Dermot O'Leary with stories of the anniversary do. She kept them brief but amusing. She counted out Donna's fee, declined the offer of a drink and allowed him to escort her to the side of the stage to watch Marie's performance. On the other side of the wall, Donna, the real Marie, had been going through her numbers. A rallentando here, a key change there – it was just like old times. Marie was in her element. She hoped both Michael and Donna would be proud of her.

Nervously the two friends waited beside the stage, both scared of either revealing their true identities. 'The Newry Beats' played a few opening numbers before introducing, 'all the way from The Trocadero, Belfast' their guest singer, Donna. To applause and wolf whistles, Marie walked onto the stage. She feared that someone at any minute would shout out, "That's not Donna Murphy. That's Michael Truesdale's wife," but they didn't and she got through her first set without being discovered. During the break the keyboard player gave Oonagh his card – "I hear you are looking for new acts to play gigs on the west coast. I'd be up for that. So if you like what you hear perhaps you would give us a ring."

"Certainly I'll let Michael know you are interested."

"Great. So, do you two want a drink?"

"No thanks, we're fine," said Marie, then realising what she'd done adding, "Aren't we, boss?" The manager, when present, always spoke for the client. Neither Oonagh nor Eamonn noticed for they were unaware of the Truesdale protocol.

The second set was better than the first. Slow ballads suited Marie when her voice had warmed up. The wolf whistles and applause doubled in volume and Dermot O'Leary was keen to discuss future bookings. Marie and Oonagh agreed they'd love to return 'subject to terms' and Oonagh asked Dermot to call in the afternoon as they now had a long drive home. It was not until they were on the road to Belfast that the girls could unleash the screams of laughter. They'd pulled it off. Marie was exhilarated. She'd not enjoyed herself so much in years.

"Do I really look so stern when I'm doing business?"

"Of course," laughed Oonagh, "Sure I know you better than you know yourself."

As they approached the motorway Oonagh handed over the wheel and she and Marie swapped seats. The lunchtime alcohol had worn off and Marie felt more confident in her own driving at night. She dropped Oonagh off at her house and returned home to give Michael a piece of her mind. There was no sign of his car – that piece of her mind would have to keep 'til tomorrow.

On Monday mornings, as had been her custom for the past ten years – Marie drove to University Street with the week's takings. She knew most of the staff by their first name and the usual practice was that she deposited cheques in the business account, transferred money to the home account, withdrew money from the personal account and checked the balances. Susan, her cashier that morning, greeted her with a warm smile but was unable to process all of her transactions.

"Perhaps you'd better have a word with Mr Johnson. I'll tell him you're here. I'm sure it won't take a minute."

Marie knew it would. It always did when someone said it wouldn't. Why couldn't she lodge cheques in the business account? Why were there an extra two thousand pounds in the house account and a further thousand in her savings account? What on earth was going on?

"Ah, Mrs Truesdale, take a seat. Now, I'm afraid your husband closed the business account on Friday morning. I was quite surprised as he's been banking with us for some time."

"Oh…" Marie was clearly more shocked than the bank manager had been. "What shall I do with these?"

"Well, your joint account is still open so I suggest you lodge them there for the time being until your husband issues you with further instructions… Are you all right Mrs Truesdale? Is there anything else I can help you with?"

"No, no thank you. I'm sure Michael will explain everything when he gets back."

"Have a nice day and if I can help in any way don't hesitate to call."

Standing outside the bank, Marie snatched at her breath. None of this made any sense. Had Michael planned to run off? Was the business in trouble? Why was there extra money in her account? She went back in and drew out more cash than she needed, drove her car along the Lisburn Road and headed home. A bouquet of flowers greeted her on the doorstep. It was an Interflora disaster, made to a formula somewhere in a hurry. The office phone was ringing as she struggled through the hall – it was probably Michael. She dumped the sad arrangement on the hall table and went into agony headquarters.

"Hello, Marie Truesdale speaking."

"Oh hi Marie, just calling to say that, as of today Eric and I are no longer available for bookings. Sorry for any inconvenience, thanks for a wonderful eight years. Hope you like the flowers – Take care."

The rapid-fire delivery barely allowed Marie to gather her thoughts. She tried calling Pizzazz back but the line was constantly engaged. The card in the hall arrangement was just as bleak. "Thank you for everything, best wishes, Suzy and Eric, Pizzazz." They'd seemed quite happy on Friday night – it just didn't add up.

The turn of the key in the door made her even more anxious – exactly what had Michael to say for himself? What was going on? It wasn't Michael who greeted her in the hallway but a red-faced Oonagh. She always looked flustered when she came over on the bus.

"Why Marie, what's wrong with you?"

"I don't quite know Oonagh – let's have a cup of tea and I'll tell you just what's happened to me this morning – you'll never believe it."

With each sip of tea and dunked ginger nut, Oonagh's incredulity grew. With each detail of the events, they worked themselves into a frenzy. Abduction, blackmail and even suicide were unwillingly considered and Marie was in an awful state when they'd finished their tea. They both went into the office to look for clues. Files were frantically searched, the bookings' diary checked, drawers opened and closed in haste but there was nothing, nothing to give them a clue to Michael's behaviour. It was Oonagh who suggested they phone the hospitals – that way at least they'd know he hadn't been in an accident. It was she who made the first call. Marie couldn't bring herself to ask the question and blamed herself for not asking it sooner. Besides Michael had planned to go away, the bank shenanigans proved that, so why something must have happened to him? She prayed it hadn't – even if at times he had been a bit of a sod he'd always believed in her. His belief, unlike her mother's, was not based on self-interest or self-promotion. He'd groomed her on stage and off, he'd made her a good performer and a sound businesswoman – at least in the office. If only she'd paid more attention to the financial side she might have a clue what this was all about.

The hospitals, all too used to such enquiries, had no record of Michael Truesdale. Oonagh, drawing a blank, suggested that they call the police. It would not have been Oonagh's normal approach – she'd have called someone who knew someone to sort out her difficulties. The RUC were not welcome in her street but this was the Malone Road after all and perhaps they'd offer better assistance here. Having spent years in Holywood, Marie readily agreed to the suggestion – she had to get to the bottom of this, whatever the findings. The RUC had 'some people in the area' and promised to direct them to the Truesdale household – despite his absence Michael still had some clout.

As they waited for someone in uniform to arrive two calls added to the strangeness of the day. Donna Magee, still croaking, told how she was moving to Dublin with her boyfriend and would not be available anymore for gigs in the north, in fact she might be giving up altogether and Dermot O'Leary from The Limelight called to book Donna for a weekend gig again with The Newry Beats.

"I'll give her a weekly spot if it goes well."

"Well Donna Marie, as she now likes to be known is very much in demand – If I were you I'd commit to four dates now or you won't get her."

Oonagh learned a thing or two about negotiations that afternoon. By the end of the phone call Donna had a new billing, four secured dates and a money increase. More surprising was that Marie had agreed to do more gigs.

"You're some girl."

"Well, we've got to keep the money coming in somehow. IF something has happened to Michael, I'll be saddled with all of this. You'll have to help me Oonagh – afternoons to start with and a bit of driving. Cash in hand, how's that?"

Both women looked guilty when the RUC arrived, but they were only doing what countless Ulster women had done before – in times of strife and loss, keeping hearth and home safe.

"So, Mrs Truesdale, when exactly did your husband disappear?"

As Marie told of the anniversary party, her guilt increased. Why hadn't she reported it sooner? Why had she gone to a gig as someone else? Why hadn't she been more loving? These questions in her head made her dizzy and the fat RUC man suggested Oonagh made them all a 'nice cup of tea'. Oonagh didn't like leaving her friend with such a man but a dry throat was of no help. She returned to the lounge, tray in hand to find Marie in tears…

"I don't want to prejudge the situation Mrs Truesdale – but if I were you I'd look after number one."

"You think he's left me don't you?"

"Well, I…"

"Michael wouldn't do that, something's happened to him, somebody's got him. He wouldn't close a bank account and withdraw all that money unless he was forced to."

"Now, now Mrs Truesdale, calm yourself… Did your husband have any threatening calls? Did he seem under more pressure than normal recently? Has his behaviour changed in any way?"

The negative answers to these questions only made Marie more concerned. Oonagh showed the constable to the door, "Well, we have the car's detail, that's a start. We'll look into it but it looks to me like your friend's husband's done a runner. There's a lot of that goes on, you know, see you love."

Oonagh didn't tell Marie exactly what the policeman had said – it would be of no consolation. She borrowed Marie's car and drove home for more clothes. She'd stay there until Michael got back – whatever his condition.

Marie was busy in the office when Oonagh returned. Fortunately the calls were all positive: managers confirming bookings, venues enquiring after acts and two hours of hectic activity had taken Marie's mind off the start of the day and the horrible RUC visit. She had to keep on top of things for Michael, for herself. He couldn't have left her in the lurch. He couldn't have gone without saying goodbye. She was sure he'd be in touch very soon. In the office talking with his clients she felt close to him – Oonagh had to virtually drag her back to the kitchen for some dinner. Both ate little and worried much. Together they decided that no one should know. Michael was simply 'away on business'. Oonagh almost faltered when Mrs Downey called and caught her off guard but she stayed loyal to her friend. Besides Mrs Downey always seemed to look down at her and she was delighted to be able to keep a secret from her once again. It was easy to lie on the telephone – they did it all the time in the office. For the outside world it would be business as usual but Marie only ventured out when she really had to. Oonagh did most of the cooking and shopping. She enjoyed taking care of someone again and Marie was no bother at all.

Marie had never doubted Michael. Twelve years she'd known him and in all that time she had no reason to doubt him. Her mother had never been that keen but she liked the trappings that his business provided and had learned, over the years, to hold her tongue. Moira Downey wanted a grandchild and so her silent judgement was not altruistic. If she nagged at her daughter Marie would simply dig in her heels.

It was true that Michael seldom explained himself but even if he had to go away he always left a note pinned to the board in the kitchen or scribbled on a pad in the office near the telephone. The absence of any such note worried Marie. She knew in her heart That Michael would return in time but she couldn't help wondering why he had gone in the first place. At least she wasn't on her own. It was great to have Oonagh around – someone who understood anxiety.

They took turns at answering the phones. Oonagh quite liked saying, "Truesdale Talent. How may I help you?" Sometimes she couldn't and had to pass the phone to Marie but she soon learned her way round the card index of clients, the fee structure and their diary. Marie talked with the acts, as she always had and when they asked after Michael, said only that he was away on one of his trips. She thought Oonagh must have got the bookings wrong when Shebang's' father called to query that night's venue. Marie took over the call in an attempt to pacify the irate father of five overweight girls – "So where the feck are we playing tonight?

Michael's got us booked at Ross' Point and you say we're in Portrush."

"Give me half an hour Seamus and I'll call you straight back."

Marie checked the bookings sheet; there was no note of a Ross' Point gig – according to the schedule that Oonagh had checked Shebang was billed at Kelly's. She phoned Kelly's to confirm that they were due to appear that night – "Oh no love, their dad's been taken ill and they're cancelling all their gigs in the north."

"This is Marie Truesdale of Truesdale Talent; can I ask you who told you that?"

"Certainly love, your husband Michael called yesterday – pity you have no replacement acts. Good luck with the new business."

Marie was not aware of any new business and Shebang's' father was far from ill – what exactly was Michael up to? Oonagh phone the Bay Hotel at Ross' Point and sure enough 'The Northern sensation – She bang' were playing that evening. Marie called Seamus with the news.

"Great – tell Michael to sort out his bloody booking system once and for all." Seamus hung up. His aggressive manner shocked Marie. He always suffered from small man syndrome – his five daughters, six if you counted the one at the special school – a desperate attempt to prove himself someone of stature.

"Michael's up to something Oonagh and he's taking all the acts with him." She started on the phone, double confirming that day's confirmations. She talked to managers and clients – the cheques would be made payable to Mrs Marie Truesdale – whatever he was up to she and Oonagh were not going to starve.

By the day of 'Donna Marie's' second booking at 'The Limelight' there was still no word from Michael. Marie felt nauseous all morning. Should she call the police? Why hadn't they got more news? What had she done to make him leave her? Oonagh too was living in turmoil. Michael had been so helpful when she'd had to fill in all those forms for the Northern Ireland Office – how could someone who had been so considerate do something like this to poor Marie? Poor Marie was thinking exactly the same thing. As she did the lunch dishes and Marie once again leafed through some old paperwork for clues of her husband's whereabouts, Oonagh reflected on her own disappeared men. They had no choice when they vanished; there was no time for goodbyes. Michael Truesdale had had the time but had chosen to say nothing. Oonagh scolded herself for such an evil thought. If Michael had been snatched by the provost or the UVF – he could be lying in an unmarked field, his body never to be recovered. But had he phoned Sligo from the grave? No, no, Michael was alive and putting her best friend through too much pain.

"Right," she announced, drying cloth still in hand, "We've got to find Donna Marie."

Marie wasn't at all sure about this but, as Oonagh said, "What harm can it do?"

"Besides, I quite like being you for an evening – it makes me feel in control." The teasing and backcombing commenced again and by four o'clock Donna Marie walked down the hall in a red sequinned skirt and top ready for another night in 'The Limelight'.

Marie had leant Oonagh a dress and shoes – "You'll look more the part." The shoes were too high for driving so Oonagh had placed them on the back seat preferring to wear her everyday flats for the drive to Newry. Both seemed more nervous than on their previous visit. Could they really pull it off again? Would Donna Marie be a one-gig wonder? The first time had been exhilarating but, with the added worry over Michael their thoughts were as confused as Donna Marie's identity.

They needn't have worried – Dermot O'Leary greeted them like long lost friends – he provided them with baskets of scampi and chips and a complimentary seven up. The band were equally pleased – Donna, Donna Marie as she now was gave them that much needed bit of glamour – two bald blokes, a salt'n'pepper fellow and a red haired and faced bass player is hardly a draw – however good the music. With Donna Marie, 'The Newry Beats' had sex appeal and all four lads rose to the occasion. Dermot made out the cheque to 'Mrs Marie Truesdale' between the sets and Oonagh, having checked the amount, placed it in her shoulder bag – on loan from Marie.

The elation they had experienced on the first night was missing but Marie had performed better and they were more relieved than excited on the drive back to Belfast. The following morning, they were rudely awakened by a land rover braking outside the house and a sharp knock on the door. Both in dressing gowns, it had been after one o'clock after all when they got in, they went downstairs. Marie opened the door and ushered a Constable Brannigan into the sitting room. They were too busy fearing the worst to notice he was on their side – a rarity in the force.

"Mrs Marie Truesdale?"

"Yes, that's me Officer," replied Marie.

"We've found your husband's car in Dunmurry. If you come with us now you can identify it and bring it back – if you have some spare keys."

"Yes I think Michael keeps some…"

"Oh and the lads found this note, addressed to you. Sorry we had to open it but, under the circumstances, I'm sure you'll understand."

Shaking Marie took the paper from the stranger and unfolded it as Oonagh stood by her side.

"I'm sorry Marie that it has come to this, all my love, Michael."

Marie let out a guttural sob – had Michael planned to kill himself in Dunmurry? What did it all mean?

Oonagh drove with Marie to collect the car. It was odd to be tailing a land rover – not at all the normal procedure. M The boot of the car had been blown open – a policeman helped Marie and Oonagh bang it shut but there was no sign of any damage, apart from the smashed side window of the missing radio. Marie looked under the car before getting into the driver's seat. With a deep breath she turned the key in the ignition and closed her eyes. On opening them she was still in the same place and the engine was ticking over. Well, that was a relief – these days you never knew what would happen when you started your car. All the way to Derryvolgie Avenue Oonagh tailed her friend. So, there was a note and a car but no husband. In her heart Oonagh knew that Michael had left on purpose. She didn't know why, perhaps they never would. In the car in front Marie was going over ten years of marriage. What had she done to drive Michael away? "I'm sorry Marie that it has come to this." What was he saying, what had the marriage come to? Five days ago she was happy. They were planning a holiday in Spain. Now she was driving his car back to the home she might have to leave. Marie knew nothing about mortgage repayments, insurance or income tax. She reprimanded herself for lack of knowledge. What the hell would her parents say when all this came to light. She cold hears her mother's "Well, I never liked him" reverberating round the kitchen as her Mellor's kitchenware was ritually abused. But what if none of this was Michael's choice? What if some of his cross border dealings had backfired? What if he'd been the victim of an extortion racket? She decided, there and then, to visit the Police Station and see someone in charge.

As they ate baked potatoes and curry, which Oonagh had collected from Spud-u-like in University Street, Marie announced her plans. She'd go down to the Police Station off Oxford Street and demand more answers. Oonagh offered to go down with her but Marie needed her to keep the business ticking over. She left at two o'clock and Oonagh, mug of tea in hand, began her office duties.

The after lunch period was always slow. The turns having just woken up always had an afternoon nap after their late breakfast. Things really only picked up after three and was on a busy day went mad until seven. Oonagh was preoccupied with thoughts of Marie for much of the afternoon but still managed to sound fairly chirpy when on the phone. She dealt with two payment enquiries and a wrong number before his call.

"Truesdale Talent, how may I help you?"

"Marie, it's me…"

"Actually Michael," there was no mistaking the voice; "it's Oonagh, where the hell are you?"

"Can I speak with Marie please?"

He sounded aggressive – just as well Marie wasn't here, though Oonagh.

"She's not here, Michael, she's," Oonagh paused not knowing whether to tell of the police visit or not, "she's sorting out some bank stuff."

"Shit… Well tell her I'm fine, I didn't mean it to end like this but I've had to go away. Tell her to get on with her life and that I loved her."

"But Michael, how can she contact you?"

"She can't."

As unexpectedly as it had come, the call ended. Neatly Oonagh re-wrote every word from the scribbled sheet that she'd scribed during the call. She knew that Marie would want every sentence, pause and breath – they'd be analysing that for hours. Oonagh called the operator – could they trace the call? The sharp lady at the Exchange was of no help. She paced round the office and then eventually found the number of the police station in the well-thumbed directory. Efficient but abrupt, the policeman couldn't trace a 'Marie Truesdale' so Oonagh gave him a message asking Marie to call home. She waited all afternoon by the telephone, re-running Michael's call in her head, but Marie never rang.

As the key turned in the front door, Oonagh pulse raced. Before Marie had a chance to take the key from the lock, Oonagh blurted out, "He's called."

Marie had had a terrible time at the police station. The two men were efficient but she could tell they thought that Michael had done a runner. The note she'd just been given proved them right. He had decided to go. He had decided to end their relationship. He had left her up shit creek. Marie slumped onto the stairs. She hadn't even bothered to remove her coat. For the first time since the boys' funeral, Oonagh understood why people become choked with emotion. She didn't know what to say to her dearest friend. In silence she slumped onto the floor and stared at her.

Marie rushed into the office when the phone rang.

"Michael, Michael."

But it wasn't her errant husband – it was the Europa Hotel confirming a booking on Friday. Oonagh took over the call as Marie sat in a chair and sobbed. At eleven o'clock the following morning the concerned parents arrived. Moira Downey, in a no-nonsense dress and cardigan was first through the door. She deposited two boxes of Bells cakes on the hall table and hugged Marie with an 'I told you' so over shoulder gaze at Oonagh. She helped James Downey unload the meat and potato pies, the groceries and the flowers from the car. "What a carry on" was his only greeting. Secretly he was jealous of Michael. Imagine being able to disappear like that. He'd longed to do something similar when Marie was at the Sacred Heart but he simply didn't have the balls. Moira Downey had kept a firm grip on those since senior school and there was no way she'd have let him go so early. Perhaps, in private, Marie, his dearest daughter was just like her mother. Perhaps Michael Truesdale sought his private pleasures elsewhere. He was too wiley to have been abducted – he had eyes on the back of his head that one.

"Let's have a cup of tea and see what's to be done."

Moira Downey never knew what to do, thought Oonagh, just as well Mr Downey, the practical one, was here too. Oonagh made for the office but within minutes James Downey came to fetch her. She had a wise head on her shoulders and had been through a lot worse than a disappearing act. Besides she had taken Michael's call and may be able to give a little insight into how he sounded.

Over and over they filled the teapot, over and over they analysed the party and its aftermath – they couldn't find any logic in the Truesdale departure.

"Right James," said Moira after endless cyclical delectation, "what's to be done?"

With Oonagh, James rooted through the house things, arranged an appointment at the bank, called a friend who was a solicitor near the law courts and planned his daughter's future. He'd always been good with money – even if it wasn't his own. The meetings arranged, all for the following day, James set about catching up with Oonagh. Life had lined her but in that face James saw the same uncertain girl he'd once taken on holiday to Newcastle. The gratitude, simplicity and honesty he'd sensed when her parents delivered her to their door was still present and he knew, unlike his wife, that if Marie were to get through this she'd need to rely on this little girl who had seen too much.

Marie and Moira held hands in the kitchen – the one silent, the other unleashing a monologue of contempt. She let her mother go on and on. She knew the criticisms were out of love and fear. Soon Dad would return and restore order. He'd sort it all out, without malice.

Michael had said he'd loved her – even on the telephone, she had proof of that in her hand but had she ever really known him? Yes she loved him but why had he spent so much time on the road? Why hadn't they had children? How could she manage on her own?

As James and Oonagh entered, the one to reheat the meat and potato pies, the other to relieve his wife Marie realised her mistake. She wasn't really on her own. Oonagh would help her through. There was a business to run, a public to face. In that brief moment she realised just how like her mother she'd become and that realisation pained her. At least her mother had kept her husband – she'd failed to do even that.

Oonagh watched her friend struggle with a lunch that once would have pleased her. The pain of absence she knew all too well – those hours before she had identified her boys had been agony. Much of that anguish lived on inside her but she knew her boys were in heaven, she knew they'd loved her. Michael Truesdale had left too many questions behind him and for that, thought Oonagh, despite her religion, he should never be forgiven. He'd made Marie doubt herself; Marie, always confident, always a performer, always just right. What had he done to her? What had she done to deserve this? They'd have to find him and get some answers. That's what they decided that evening on their own.

Chapter Eleven

With each day's absence, Donna Marie grew in strength. Marie herself still crumbled away inside longing for the truth but with Oonagh help the business side of things was maintained. The acts that had departed were never on the same circuit and only occasionally were there problems with the mortgage payments. The girls settle into a routine. Wednesday 'til Saturday, Oonagh stayed at Derryvolgie while for the rest of the week she remained at home. In this way they both had companionship and loneliness in equal measure. Oonagh Donnelly now managed Donna Marie. As a child Oonagh had been bad at lying, her wee innocent face always told the truth, so the evenings of deception were difficult for her. She couldn't bring herself to confessing them – it was a half-truth after all; she was looking after her friend, making sure everything was right for her; but deception is deception and each time she was introduced as Marie her stomach churned. No amount of Alka-Seltzer could quell the guilt and eventually Donna Marie was 'under new management'. Marie liked the arrangement. It gave her friend much needed confidence and the financial payments, begun as charity, became formal and clear-cut. Oonagh was on a percentage.

So, content with how Oonagh dealt with her alter ego, Marie decided that two of the new signings should be hers – a disco dancing duo 'Sparkle' who needed polish and a country and western band 'Deep south' four farmers from Dervock. Of the three, Donna Marie was the most popular, gigging two or three times a week.

At every gig they scoured the audience, eavesdropped backstage for talk of the long lost acts but at no point did they get a lead on the whereabouts of the missing husband.

The Parish Hall had burned down all by itself. There was no terrorist act, no catholic-hating incendiary, just a faithful servant who had reached the end of its days; an old oil heater that warmed the vestry in winter. Various committees had had fund-raisers for years and at last the Victorian Church was replaced by a multi-purpose rotunda where civil duty and worship could be conducted. The steeple of the old building sealed and intact stood as a reminder of the past and beside it a circular postmodern structure held the future. It was inward rather than upward looking – a building reflecting the problems of the town in which it stood. Nevertheless a grand opening ceremony was called for and the entertainments committee was formed.

Father Fuscoe had had dealings with 'Truesdale Talent' in the past – they always delivered and at a fair price. Pizzazz had been a particular favourite at his 'Night at the races' and somewhere in his barren bedroom was a card with the manager's number. He called before the meeting – after all there were only so many recitations from pensioners one could listen to. The re-opening of St Colmcille's was to be a grand affair and, once the locals had done their bit surely some professionals were needed. Billed as an evening of thanksgiving – it was really a night of dedication, supper and entertainment and, new to the parish, Father Fuscoe needed to impress.

A woman answered the telephone. Michael Truesdale was 'away on business' but she handled most of the acts and seemed quite helpful. Donna Marie seemed to fit the bill and, as it was such a prestigious event the lady suggested a new band, just arrived from America – Deep South. Now that would really impress the Bishop. St Colmcille's entertainment committee were less enthusiastic. What was wrong with Geraldine O'Connor's harp playing, why couldn't Paddy McMahon's choir sing 'The Age of Aquarius' and surely the girls' school and its drama group could do something in leotards? Kieran Fuscoe was least keen on the last option – their anti-abortion play let – performed at Mass one Sunday Morning was womb-crunchingly awful. The chubby girls in stretched Lycra were no adverts for life. As ever, a compromise was reached, and Kieran got his way. Geraldine would harp play on arrival, Paddy McMahon's choir would learn a new number and Donna Marie and Deep South would be the post supper entertainment.

Donna Marie was not so keen. Singing with a house band was one thing, but fronting for four farmers was completely different. It was the first disagreement that Marie and Oonagh had. "But I've done the booking, and they're all very keen."

"Or deluded," quipped Marie. "Just how long have these Dervock boys been playing together?"

"Years and they're really very good."

"Says who?"

"Well, me and their father."

"Shit!"

Deep South arrived in Derryvolgie Avenue on Wednesday morning. *Four handsome big lads,* thought Marie to herself as she watched them unload the van and set up in the lounge.

To Oonagh's surprise Marie suggested a fry-up to set them up for the day. She seldom cooked in the mornings but busied herself in the kitchen while Oonagh distributed sheet music and worked out where they were going to sleep. As they sat round the breakfast table Marie and Oonagh realised how much they missed male company. Neither communicated these thoughts. They didn't need to; it was obvious as they passed round ketchup and bread.

Versatility and compromise were not naturally found in Dervock and the lads stayed true to their birthplace for much of the day. Gerry on keys and Eoin on lead guitar were used to doing the singing and it was strange for them to have a woman in the band. Marie found them stubborn and not that musical. They could play the stuff their way and if that was your taste so be it but when Donna Marie sang she really went with it and she needed a band to go with her. Oonagh heard the disputes from the office and worried. It was good that Marie could argue her case with so much passion. The boys were no pushovers and she knew the arrangement was ideal.

As Deep South sank deep pints on the corner of the Lisburn Road, Oonagh and her second vodka and tonic listened to Marie rail against them. Despite protestations she cooked the lads a late breakfast and rehearsed 'til late the following day. By teatime they had a running order and a show.

On the Friday morning they transported the equipment across town – the four lads that is. Oonagh and Marie drove across after lunch for a run-through.

The hall was impressive. Father Fuscoe was there to greet them. Blotchy faced, he was younger than Oonagh imagined –

he reminded her of the priest at school, the one that Miss Slevin loved. He wasn't as tall as Father Fullerton but he too was a hen-pecked only son.

"We're so glad you've agreed to do this. It's a very special night for the Parish and it's lovely to have some real professionals."

Oonagh suspected that, had he not been a priest, Father Fuscoe would never have married. He was a closet entertainer. At least with the church there was a captive audience and a divine system of advance bookings.

As Oonagh thanked him for the opportunity and pocketed the cheque, Marie and the boys began a sound check. It was great to see her in control. Bossing the boys in the band and always getting her way. What would Michael Truesdale have made of all this, wondered Oonagh? He'd never really wanted Marie to perform. He didn't say as much but in the two years that Oonagh had observed him, he'd given his wife little encouragement in any area. Oonagh didn't really miss him and, as she watched her friend strut her songs she wondered if Marie really did, deep down, where things mattered.

They were due back at the hall at six thirty. The boys set off for a look around town and Oonagh and Marie drove back to the house for rest and transformation.

Rarely had St Colmcille's seen such an occasion. Certainly it was the largest event that Father Fuscoe had ever organised and, as much of the onus was on him, his skin reddened accordingly. He was thrilled with his talent – Michael Truesdale was not an easy man to crack but he had given St Colmcille's one of his hottest acts and at a discount price. Perhaps the man had mellowed. Rory, the Fuscoe cousin knew Michael of old. He'd done dealings with him in the seventies but the show band killings had ended Rory's musical ambition and, although he still had some contacts, Rory managed a decent bar in the wrong part of town. Father Fuscoe was looking forward to showing his cousin just how well he was doing. Being in charge on the entertainment committee and the parish priest, he'd wangled two tickets by way of thanks.

In the flat above the bar Rory's wife was not keen. Since his depression she'd tried to keep Rory away from the music scene. Sure, a few memories with mates in the bar was fine but the whole business side of things was too painful. He'd booked the lads that gig, he'd planned their route, and he'd pulled out at the last minute as Carmel was in labour. Everything was premature that evening; her baby, the band's remorse, his new boy's death. He couldn't have stopped the bastards shooting his mates, he couldn't have given his dead son life but his guilt remained constant.

In the bedroom of her family-less home, Marie made Donna-Marie hers. Oonagh had excelled in the flicking and the new chiffon outfit, bat-winged and pastel matched flick for line. It was a church event after all and sequins seemed a little too flash. Why had they decided on taking a taxi? Oonagh had wanted to drive but Marie had insisted – the lads could give them a lift back in the van and it was about time Oonagh let her hair down. She'd worked so hard for her friend, had kept her sane and even the books, and at last was starting to balance.

In a crowded booth in the Crown bar Deep South were on their second pint of Guinness. They were glad of a break from the women. Oonagh was tough but Marie as Donna Marie was a right taskmaster. Still, they had learnt a lot from the past few days and concluded that they might have a musical future after all.

The audience arrived early. Apart from the visiting dignitaries, no one had allocated seats. That way they could ignore health and safety and squeeze in some extra seats as required. Posters in Andersonstown proclaiming 'Tickets available at the door' would generate an overspill and extra money for the funds.

The men and women of the parish were on hand to meet and greet. Despite the lack of speed in Speedy cabs Marie and Oonagh arrived in good time. The Dervock Boys were already there. Oonagh thought they'd been drinking – there was no mistaking that peaty smell but she decided against confrontation. She thought it odd that Father Fuscoe was spending so much time backstage – surely he should be out with his Parishioners?

Deep South and Donna Marie waited patiently. All through the prayers, all through the strangled slaughter of Ave Maria, all through the harp playing, the pubescent soloists and the bouquets. They were still waiting when the supper was served. The lads ate several platters of sandwiches – Oonagh was delighted – that would soak up some of the Guinness at least.

Donna Marie was ravenous, but Marie was too nervous to allow her to eat anything.

"And now everyone, a real treat – push back the chairs and prepare to welcome Donna Marie and Deep South." With single-handed applause, the other hands occupied with chair manoeuvres – the St Colmcille's assembled greeted that evening's professional performers. Energy fuelled by Guinness and suppressed longing burst onto the stage. Rory Fuscoe had been almost asleep until then. Had it not been for Carmel's elbow he might have drifted off completely. The girl in the band seemed familiar. He'd heard that sound before. Not those songs but that voice. The harder she sang, the harder he thought.

It wasn't from his schooldays – he'd have kept in touch with her surely – so what was her story. On the road he'd met hundreds of women – she might have been a groupie. Eoin would know – they'd pop backstage after the first set and ask her. By the look of things Carmel was in no form for dancing.

The backstage area behind the hall was purgatory. Needy girls and forlorn boys fought over the leftover sandwiches, Irish dancers huddled together like old women wishing they'd brought a change of clothes for the dancing and causing between the mayhem, raffle tickets in hand was Eoin Fuscoe.

"Well Father, how's it going?"

"Not bad at all Carmel, not bad at all."

"Here, let me do the rounds with them and you can do a bit of catching up."

Carmel grabbed the pink books of tickets and set off for the hall –

"Father, what's the prize and how much is a book?" It was typical of Carmel to jump in feet first and ask questions later thought Rory – that's how they married in the first place.

"A weekend in Jury's in Dublin and a pound."

"Jesus, father, I'll take five books myself."

That was also typical, thought Rory.

"It's a great night; you must be chuffed with yourself."

"Well Rory, it's not all to do with me."

They both, being cousins, knew this to be a lie.

"That girl's got a great voice – where's she from?"

"Well, I booked her with Truesdale Talent – that woman over there's her manager. Why don't you ask her?"

There was no need to ask. The girl on stage was all too familiar. He'd done a gig with her a long time ago and the band was just getting known. As a bass player he hadn't paid that much attention to her at first but as her voice rang around the Queen's Court he soon grew interested. So, she was still singing. Rory was surprised that Michael allowed a wife of his to appear on stage. He was a jealous type – but maybe he too had mellowed with age.

"She's doing a grand job, your girl. How's her auld man?"

"Oh well."

"Now come on, I bet you'd fancy a weekend for two in Dublin – they're only a pound a book."

As Oonagh fumbled for her purse to appease the seller Marie and the band arrived backstage. Before Oonagh had a chance to intercept Rory was off.

"Marie Truesdale, how the hell are you?"

Thrilled by her own singing and breathless from her public acknowledgement Marie took a while to respond.

"You don't remember me do you – Rory Fuscoe – one time bass player with the Florida show band."

The room silenced a little when the band was mentioned. So that was Rory Fuscoe – the bass player that got away. Marie had heard Michael mention him often enough 'Lucky bastard' he often said, but there was little luck evident in the eyes that undressed Donna Marie.

"I was there at your first gig – we were the house band at the Court in Bangor. Michael wangled you in as a favour. I'm amazed you are still singing. Christ was it that bad?" Even the Dervock Four laughed nervously.

"No, but I thought he married you off… How is the old bastard?"

Oonagh arrived at her side just in time for the truth.

Before they could say no, Marie, her manager and the band were following a blue Volkswagen to McDaid.

Oonagh smiled to herself. Old man McDaid had passed on years ago. His only son still in the north had no interest in bar work and the business had been sold. Like Nuala, the Fuscoe's had kept the name – it was McDaid's bar and always would be.

As the band sipped room temperature Guinness – Marie told Carmel and Rory the truth. She felt safe with them. Like Oonagh they'd been close to death and knew the importance of getting on with it.

Marie unwrapped her fears. In his heart, Rory knew that Michael was alive – the removal of funds proved it. Besides Truesdale had enough links with both sides to get him out of any bother. Oonagh laughed at how meticulous the plan had been. For months they'd been gigging and there were still no leads.

"It's been tough, especially with so many acts giving up and moving at such short notice to Dublin."

"Like who?" asked Carmel nervously.

"Well," replied Oonagh. "Donna for a start, the Pizzazz."

"What was that?" asked Rory

"Pizzazz – they gave up too."

"That's not some blind bloke and a dodgy bird that needs a good seeing to?"

"Yes it is," laughed Marie.

"They've not given up – I'm sure they're on some flyer we got."

Rory went behind the bar and re-emerged with a box file.

"It's where I keep all the brewery crap," he rummaged impatiently through the box.

"There you go, 'Sligo Festival of Music'. There they are…"

Pizzazz – would you look at the fuckers? No wonder other acts had still to be announced, thought Oonagh

"Well, well," said Marie, "fancy an august trip to Sligo lads?"

On their third pint, and having no idea what prompted the invitation the guys agreed a why not?

"Why don't we make a weekend of it too Carmel – you've been saying we need a break and anyway, it may nail that bastard Truesdale once and for all – no offence, Marie."

"None taken, Rory."

Oonagh was somewhat surprised at Marie's lack of offence, but Marie had lived under Michael's shadow for too long and although that shadow had disappeared under dubious circumstances she was growing to appreciate the freedom that his absence gave.

Strange, how the buzz of a successful performance makes one uncharacteristically decisive. With a harvey wallbanger hangover Marie wondered what she had got herself into. Oonagh was already busy with enquiries and arrangements by the time Marie felt human. If they couldn't be paid as Truesdale they could be paid in cash or one of the lads from 'Deep South' could be the payee. Their cheques would take longer to clear, Dervock was hardly Belfast and she'd have to fess up as to what Marie was at but that was a small price to pay if it led them to Michael Truesdale. How to sell the act that was the problem. She couldn't risk booking as the Truesdale Talent agency – someone somewhere would make the connection – it would all need to be done another way. The first call from 'Downey Enterprises' was difficult but thanks to a bloke called Eamonn from the Sligo Herald Oonagh soon had a couple of possible dates and venues to explore. Pizzazz were at the Cliff Hotel. It would be too risky to get a booking there – fifty percent of that group could easily recognise them. When Marie thought to enquire just what exactly was going on Oonagh put the phone down on their third confirmed booking? Towards the end of the week Moira Downey called with news.

"What on earth were you thinking of Marie – you're all over the Andersonstown News. What has got into you – a reputable married woman singing with a band of Americans, and they've got your name wrong."

So that's what it was all about – Moira Downey's daughter had become a misprint. How funny that her Mother, who had so longed to put her daughter on the stage, and herself if possible, should be embarrassed. It was the nature of the entertainment that bothered her. An opening of a Church hall, however grand, could hardly be claimed as a 'professional engagement'. *If only she'd seen some of the places we've played,* thought Marie, *she'd soon change her view.* At that moment, Marie and her Mother grew further apart. She'd longed to tell her of the Sligo plan, about meeting Rory – that blast from the past, but the Holywood snob on the other end of the phone would only have given a negative reaction and that was the last thing Marie required. Sometimes, it is the parents who disappoint, not the children.

"Oonagh and I are going away for a few days at the end of the month – would you and Dad like to mind the house for me?"

This was her olive branch, but as soon as she'd extended it, it lost its value. Her mother had so many things to do – what with the festival, the Holywood Players, St Patrick's new hall committee and the bottle stall that it was agreed that James would pop in a couple of times to check up on things. *Good old Dad,* thought Marie. *What would either of us do without him?*

With just two weeks to prepare, Rory and Carmel's had provided the ideal rehearsal venue. Here, among oak-stained wood panels and chewing gum patterned carpets, they practised for the tour; that's what they called the week in Sligo. 'Downey Enterprises' or to be more accurate Oonagh, with Marie's, approval, naturally, had given Rory a good deal. The band even let him try out a few numbers with them. Carmel, who initially had not been too keen on his rekindling of the past, saw his eyes light up as when they first met and had concluded that, as this was the man she'd married, she'd best accept it. Marie loved the nights in McDaid's. She felt part of the place and this security allowed her to interact with the crowd and to try more home-grown music on them. Her approach, somewhere between Dana and Philomena Begley pleased the regulars and even before the two weeks of rehearsal were up they'd got a fortnightly gig at Rory's.

Accommodation in Sligo was proving a problem. "Deep South," said they could kip in the van, "after all, it's only for a week," and purchased sleeping bags to show they meant it. Rory and Carmel said they'd make their own arrangements. He had more contacts from the past that he wanted to look in on and she thought it best if contact with Marie remained 'purely professional'.

The primitive building off Royal Avenue – jokingly referred to as 'The Northern Irish Tourist Board' offered little assistance. Only the most determined of tourists made it to the North – those on a peace mission to Corrymeela or on a teaching exchange from some other third world country. Oonagh and Marie rang the bell several times before they gained access to the office. It was dimly lit and very quiet.

"Good morning," said a rotund girl who was no advert for the Ulster Fry. "What can I do for you?"

The girls explained their needs. Several brochures for B&B in the land of a thousand smiles were provided and a map with a leprechaun on it was purchased but the globular Frankie was sceptical about them finding anything – "There's a music

109

festival, you see, which is very popular with Americans these days."

These two didn't look like Irish musicians. One was quite well spoken – when she was allowed to do the talking. Why on earth would two women like that want to holiday in Sligo?

Frankie knew all about lesbians – she'd met a couple on a tourist board exchange; Northern women with sharp haircuts and even sharper tongues. She'd had to sit with them at lunch on the first day and it quite put her off her 'toad in the hole'. They thought, from her unhappy size and spare make up that she, despite being from Northern Ireland, was one of their sisters. Frankie couldn't imagine being related to anything worse. Still her training had taught her to treat anyone who made it through the taped door warmly and she did her best for the two local girls seeking escape.

Over coffee and an apple square near the security barriers the two friends considered their options. Couldn't they just take potluck? Wasn't it better to ask someone locally? Perhaps Rory could help them. On their second coffee they decided to book somewhere for the first night, if they could, and take it from there. Oonagh took a bus back to the house; her aim, to do just that and Marie went into town to pick up some last minute bits and pieces.

She'd just finished in bras and was heading to the till when Marie bumped into Carmel in nightdresses. Marks and Spencer was new to Belfast and currently the shop of the moment.

"Och, Jesus, how are you? Have you sorted out where you're staying yet?"

Marie replied that Oonagh as ever was 'on the case' and asked if they'd managed to find accommodation.

"I've taken nothing to do with it. I wanted to stay in a B&B for the craic but me man wants to relive old times. I've told him we're not staying in a shithole."

"It'll be a laugh, in any case, and Christ do I need some of that." Carmel remembered what the trip was all about and scolded herself for appearing so negative.

"Is he bringing the guitar?"

"Now Marie, what do you think? You'll probably be singing with a new five piece band by the end of the week."

The final 'rehearsal gig' at McDaid's was electric. The band was tighter than ever and as Carmel distributed a tray of drinks they all sat down in the sitting room to finalise the plans. Oonagh thought it best that Rory acted as tour manager – it was easier for him to control the four boys and, as he'd been to Sligo before he planned the route, suggested a lunch venue and several rendezvous points for the stay.

"It's no point going in convoy – what with these two in the flash car and you lot in that bloody van – so let's meet up for a good feed at the Four Winds Hotel at one o'clock. They do a decent carvery – I know you lads like your grub."

Oonagh was excited. She'd never been away in a group before – well, not since she was at school and the combinations of freedom and the safety blanket of organisation appealed to her. As they drove back home their minds wandered. Would they track down Michael? Would Carmel give her man enough rope? Would the Dervock Four stick to their Guinness rations? With these and other questions left unanswered, Marie and Oonagh slept soundly, dreaming of their long lost men. It was cloudy but not unpleasant at nine o'clock on the Sunday morning they set off. Like teenagers setting out on an adventure they'd been up early. Of course they left most of the packing till the last minute – "just in case things get creased." They need not have had such concerns as, on the previous evening Oonagh had packed an iron, some hangers and a water spray in the car for that very reason. By six thirty the 'should I take' debate had started. It was more difficult for Marie – she had to pack for Donna as well. Oonagh's case was organised but small – she didn't wish to take up too much room in the car. She laid out her special outfits – of which there were two in the back seat and Marie piled Donna Marie's stage clothes on top. It looked like an end of season sale at Renee Meneeley's – Frank Usher struggling for pole position with Mondi and Escada. They had no idea what the venues were like – Oonagh had agreed to pop in to suss them out on the afternoon of the shows to give Donna Marie a fighting chance. Although Michael's car was faster and repaired, thanks to the gigs at McDaid's they couldn't risk taking it. So Marie had spent much of Saturday vacuuming her run-around. She'd hand washed it while Oonagh was at home packing. The jet wash at the end of the road always left streaks – the wee boy never chamoised off the water properly. Elbow deep in suds, she'd thought of those rare days when she helped her dad wash the car. Her mother never allowed her to help – "little girls shouldn't be seen washing cars in the street." So, while her mother was out shopping James and she would take advantage of good weather and her absence and have a good laugh.

Oonagh enjoyed the first part of the drive – for she was the passenger. They'd agreed that as they filled two flasks with tea and put some kitchen roll in the Tupperware boxes. Marie would drive as far as the hotel and Oonagh would take the second leg.

Pleased with this arrangement, Oonagh buttered some bridge rolls that Marie filled with ham and cucumber and egg and tomato. These and a box of fifteens would provide journey refreshment.

Although they set off at nine, by the time Oonagh had familiarised herself with the route and directed them, eventually to a garage that was open on a Sunday morning it was nine thirty before they were leaving Belfast behind. Rory and Carmel were also running late – the Saturday lock in had delayed their preparations. Carmel was still packing when the girls phoned to say they were off – Rory was still in his bed, she didn't tell them that. In a Bushmills' car park four men dozed in a white van. They had plenty of time and little desire to be on the road quite so early.

Chapter Twelve

The car park of The Four Winds was witness to its success. Although bearing four stars, they had been awarded in the seventies in a desperate bid to revive the failing tourist industry and the hope that they had carried had vanished long since. As Rory had suggested, the carvery was the hotel's main attraction and as news of it had spread coach drivers included it on their routes.

Marie had to outmanoeuvre a silver estate car, two old people with walking aids and a reversing coach to claim their space. Carmel and Rory were already at the hotel entrance.

"Five past one ladies, not bad, not bad."

Sometimes Rory could be a patronising bastard, thought Oonagh. They made the smallest of talk about their journey for a further ten minutes but there was still no sign of the van.

"We should perhaps make a start and they can join us when they get here."

"Good," agreed Carmel. "Rory and I have already booked us a table."

Fear of being late had driven Rory to drive like the clappers and by the time the girls arrived they'd already spent half an hour at the bar.

"Soup or segments?" asked the curt waitress as they sat down. All chose the soup – grapefruit segments being considered part of an English breakfast. They ordered a bottle of Black Tower and a jug of iced water.

"The ice machines on the blink but we've put the jugs in the fridge so it should be cold enough. After the soup or segments, it's help yourself and eat as much as you like. Are these tables taken?"

The restaurant was filling up and the waitress, keen to keep things moving had spied a four.

"Yes, friends of ours are just coming."

"That's fine, that's fine," replied the thin-faced girl. Marie could sense that it wasn't.

The soup was Presbyterian vegetable – in the wrong place and weakened by years of tradition. It had a pale grey hue and an earthy taste that belied its lack of substance. Oonagh tried to spice it up with a good helping of salt but it still tasted insipid. No carvery could be a disappointment after this.

As the hungry quartet queued for roast pork with apple sauce, roast beef or gammon Marie gasped. The man ladling cauliflower Mornay onto his over stacked plate was wearing a jacket of Michael's. Her gasp was caused, not by the jacket itself but by the faint hope that it was her husband. The hope was quickly dispatched as the man reached across for more gravy and displayed a heavy paunch and rounded cheekbones. Michael would never have let himself go like that.

They ran out of apple sauce as Oonagh made her selection. By the time they'd replenished the steel container her roast pork was cold. She was still in the queue when 'Deep South' arrived. They were loud and apologetic and jumped straight behind her in the queue.

"We had to change a tyre on the way and then we couldn't get a space in the bloody car park. We had to leave the feckin van at the old people's home next door."

A woman with two young children tutted her disapproval. It was Sunday after all, no need for such language. Those Northerners thought they ran the place.

Puddings, like the 'soup or segments' were waitress served. Marie and Carmel chose to abstain – Oonagh had lemon meringue pie and cream and the men had apple pie a la mode – which sounded a lot daintier than it looked. Over coffee they agreed the next rendezvous point – the Cellar Bar in Jury's at nine – that way they would all get to their digs and unpack. Oonagh settled the bill; Marie had sorted out more money for Downey Enterprises and they all fought their way out of the car park.

As Oonagh steered them away from The Four Winds, the rain began. Not the ordinary spit that happens when you've hung out a spring wash but gobfuls of heavy water that railed against the windscreen and bounced off the road. Both said they'd never seen such rain and both lied; such rain was a punishment for every warm summer since childhood. It couldn't last for long. There God was a kind God after all.

The fourth tree-laden avenue led to the fourth big grey house; it was the right one, thank God. "It looks a lot like bloody Kilkeel convent," remarked Marie.

"No," laughed Oonagh. "It's a lot cheaper."

A spectre in her fifties with a craggy chin sprouting man hair greeted them.

"We thought you'd be here earlier, but you're here now so you might as well come in."

It wasn't the warmest of greetings. In the land of a thousand smiles and a thousand welcomes they fell on guesthouse one thousand and one. There was no point bringing their decent clothes inside – the car was cleaner and probably less damp. The twin bedded room was a late forties heirloom. The beds were cold.

"That's it," announced Marie. "Tomorrow we'll find somewhere else – now let's go and meet the others."

Through blankets of ever thickening pain Marie drove them to Jury's. In the passenger seat Oonagh was annoyed with herself. There hadn't been a picture in the brochure and, naively, she'd fallen for the three-line description. 'On the outskirts of Sligo' translated as 'Bloody miles away', 'impressive period building' signified 'run down wreck'. She'd apologised several times to Marie but this made matters worse.

"We'll find somewhere tomorrow, don't worry" was all she said. Oonagh knew that the chance of finding somewhere vacant and on a Sunday was slim – she'd done all the phoning round after all. They parked in the driveway of the hotel and, coats over heads, ran through the car park to the main entrance. People were in every corner of the reception area – it was a profitable night for the hotel. Three times a week 'the Irish night' with its bodhruns, fiddle players, Irish dancers and a 'traditional Irish supper'.

"Does that mean feck all?" laughed the girls – gave coach loads of Americans their sense of belonging. Several pilgrims, most of whom were on their last legs had had their dying wishes granted that very night and were refrigerated until the coach party returned from Galway. There were no Americans in the

115

Cellar bar, thank God, but it too was heaving. The damp footed girls found Rory holding court near the 'waiters only' sign. Three of Deep South were with him – supping beer as usual.

"Hello girls, what can I get you?"

"I'll have a soda water and lime thank you," replied Marie thinking of the driving rather than her throat…

"And for you Oonagh?"

"Oh, a wee Bacardi and coke."

It took ages to get the drinks, largely because of the lads' Guinness and the dressed Pimms for Carmel who'd just returned from 'the powder room'. For Carmel a proper hotel did 'dressed Pimms' with sugar round the glass and a maraschino cherry spliced with lemon and she'd decided to put Jury's to the test.

"How's your digs?" she asked Marie, her lipstick speckled with white sugar granules.

"Oh terrible, ask Oonagh."

Oonagh told of the damp grey stone, the threadbare carpets, the hairy woman at the door and the damp heavy smell that had penetrated everything. No amount of Nina Ricci could disguise it. To prove the point, Oonagh held her damp coat out to Carmel.

"Bloody hell, I see what you mean – Rory, Marie and Oonagh need your help."

Ever eager to please, particularly Marie Truesdale, Rory listened as Oonagh once again derided the B&B.

With a 'hold on a minute' he put down his pint and walked to a faraway table.

He returned a few minutes later with a smiling silver haired man who was a friend of a kind.

"Girls, this is Kieran O'Donoghue – he runs the drapers shop in the high street."

Yes, we're damp, thought Oonagh, *but purchasing new fabric is hardly the solution. And he knows everyone.*

"Well now, I wouldn't say everyone, but I do know a fair few. Now, I've a friend who's got a B&B just down the road here. It's too late to call her now but I'll be seeing her at mass tomorrow and I'll tell her you'll be round at lunchtime. Some of her regulars pulled out yesterday at short notice so she's got a few rooms going. It'll be grand, she loves the arts and she makes her own wheaten."

Marie bought Kieran O'Donoghue a wee Paddy for his kindness and asked him and his wife to come along to hear her sing. He accepted the offer and wrote Theresa Coyne's address down on a torn beer mat. Marie passed the felty note to Oonagh and bought another round.

They slept in their slips and donned damp clothes in the morning. The cooked breakfast was of wartime proportion and Oonagh couldn't wait to pay for the one night accommodation and get out of there. As they drove down the grand path it spat chips up at the windscreen – angered at the unscheduled departure. With a few hours to spare before lunchtime they took a drive into town. The rain cleared magically as they parked behind a supermarket at the kitchen of the 'Ballymoat Retreat – Closed Mondays'.

The town was being called to mass as they started the tour of the high street. Most of the shops were closed but, even with shutters down they revealed their southern traits – not only in the hand painted names – O'Reilly, O'Connor, O'Meath, but also in the painted shop fronts. Belfast was always more subdued even when owned by Catholics, looked Protestant. Bold blues and yellows here celebrated life and drew attention to the second rate merchandise. It didn't take long to find the O'Donoghue shop. Through the yellow plastic sun protectors they could see bolts of Irish tweed, suits for boys and men, shirts for funerals and fine knitwear for women. The organised array assured them that his recommendation would be sound. They gazed at the blue and white offices of 'the Sligo herald' ad read the front pages of 'this week's edition' placed in wooden framed glass cases on either side of the steps. There were two ads for the music week on each page but no mention of Donna Marie and Deep South.

"Well we did book in late," conceded Oonagh.

Theresa Coyne was expecting them. She was glad of the business. Ever since the girls had left she'd hated empty rooms. As each of her five girls had gone off, one by one to the teacher training in Dublin, never to return, she'd let their rooms and what had started off as a hobby now became her way of coping with silence. Sure, her husband, a retired insurance broker was there but he wasn't much craic. He hated gossip; he simply didn't see the need for it. Kieran O'Donoghue was a great friend. Not only was he on the committee of the Feis like herself but he also sent tourists her way so it was no surprise to her that he'd found two northern girls to fill her home.

By the time Oonagh and Marie had arrived at Beaupre, there was only one room left. Ever shrewd, Theresa had held back the twin and convinced the two Chinese students to share the double – *after all,* she thought, *it's probably what they do at home.*

"Hello, I'm Theresa, welcome to Beaupre."

The firm handshake and huge smile delighted Marie and Oonagh.

"I'll show you the room and then will you have a wee cup of tea?"

The room was cosy, not modern, but welcoming and as Marie and Oonagh unpacked their things they knew they were there for the week.

"Will you have a bit of fruit cake – homemade naturally?" The little woman was keen to appear hospitable – she'd heard what an awful time they'd had at 'Dhu varan' and was eager to give them a real Irish welcome – even though they seemed Irish themselves.

"So you're a singer?" her eyes lit up as she poured the tea.

Marie told her story, well all but the Michael part.

"And you two are friends since school, isn't that just lovely?"

They could have sat all day but Martin, her husband needed his lunch and Oonagh and Marie had to get organised for the gig. After bar snacks at Jury's Marie went back to Beaupre for a wee nap and Oonagh set off to check out the venue.

Over the next few days Oonagh became the non-singing detective. Marie was keen to trace Michael but the success of the first gig and the buzz they attracted made an absent husband, for once, a low priority.

Oonagh made friends with the man at The Chronicle, but he gave little away, drank with the manager of the 'Drop Inn' where Pizzazz were booked and had lunch with a man from the festival organising committee but still there was no sign of Michael Truesdale. She had a Filofax full of bookings (Marie thought the leather folder made Oonagh look more professional) for Donna Marie and Deep South and received enquiries about her other acts. Three agents had the booking system sewn up – or so it seemed. Event managers were thrilled to do business with someone new – they'd been booking the same old acts every year and all were fighting over the unrepresented newcomers. None of the agents worked locally – two were based in Dublin and one in Galway. Oonagh concluded, that, like herself they'd be in Sligo at some point – it was just a matter of finding their acts and hanging around. Marie thought this was a waste of time. If Michael wanted to remain hidden – no amount of hanging around would flush him out. He'd prided himself on getting out of watertight contracts and allowing his acts to represent his best interests. Sure, he'd step in if there was a crisis – but how could two wee girls from Belfast anticipate that. Between gigs, Oonagh and Marie spent much time at the beach on Ross' Point or in Jury's with Rory, Carmel and their local know-all with Theresa Coyne.

On the day after the second gig Rory and Carmel arrived late for lunch. They hadn't been to 'Rossnowlagh' for Donna Marie's latest programme – no, they'd been at Ross' Point accosting a blind man and his musical partner.

"He still manages them – he's got a Dublin office – they gave us the number but the answer phone just says he's 'away on business'."

Oonagh and Marie knew exactly what Rory was on about.

"I'd recognise that voice anywhere – but he calls himself Mihal T Dale now – the company he runs T. Dale Talent."

Marie let her chicken kiev go cold. All the worry and fear turned to anger. So, if Rory was right the bastard had simply run out on her. Oonagh left her open prawn sandwich and followed her friend back to the B&B.

"Oh Oonagh, what the hell do I do now?"

Oonagh couldn't answer Marie's question, she was going over all the possibilities in their heads. Gallivanting off to Dublin was not the answer. What was the point if he wasn't there? No, she'd call the number later and then she'd take down the address. They had one more engagement in Sligo and although they'd planned to spend a few days in Donegal perhaps they should return to Belfast and aim to take a train to Dublin on the Monday.

Marie was vomiting and on the toilet most of the day. Mrs Coyne was sympathetic but as she had no idea of the circumstances she could only assume Moira had caught a bug.

Oonagh did little to dispel this theory and sat with her friend, occasionally vomiting in sympathy.

It took a whole day's nursing to convince Marie that this was the right thing to do; a whole day's nursing to get her ready for the final Friday night gig.

Chapter Thirteen

The last gig, in Sligo town hall was to be their most prestigious. It was the penultimate night of the festival, but as drinking was curtailed on a Saturday evening by Sunday morning guilt, it was the most lucrative. They'd done well to get this venue switch. Donna Marie and Deep South had been scheduled to play at Flan O'Brien's but a last minute cancellation by a 'still to be announced' band and a roof raising reception at their last venue had secured them this much sought after slot. All that day Oonagh had kept quiet about it – she didn't want to put any more pressure on Marie but she'd forewarned the lads and told them to get there later.

Marie prepared slowly, her heart wasn't Donna-Marie's that afternoon but she didn't know to whom it belonged. She couldn't let Oonagh and the lads down. Oonagh, who was normally so enthusiastic about the transformation, today was quiet and almost mechanical. Marie decided not to read too much into it. There was quite enough turmoil in her head.

Arriving for the sound check Oonagh instantly sensed trouble. Only three of the lads were present and they all looked sheepish. "We've had a wee bit of an accident."

"A wee bit of an accident my arse" was Oonagh's response on learning that Eamonn Darcy their bass player, their only bass player, was sitting in Sligo General. He'd caught his hand in the van door after giving two local girls a lift home. "Sure it's nothing," he said to them wishing to appear like a butch boy from the north but that 'nothing' had swollen during slumber and he couldn't move his fingers in the morning; not the best of things for a guitar player. Neither Deep South nor Marie had ever seen Oonagh so angry. In truth it was a reaction to the whole Michael thing rather than to a swollen hand – all men had let her down, even Declan had got himself and her son killed.

"Right, that's it," announced Donna Marie. "We'll have to cancel."

"You must be bloody joking – sort that sound out and I'll be back in half an hour if I can find him."

Like a dying nymphomaniac in search of a last lay, Oonagh tore round Sligo looking for Rory. He and Carmel, having had a mixed grill at the Bally Moat, were shopping for souvenirs when she found them. Carmel was a little 'fucked off' to have her lovely afternoon curtailed. She'd feared that this would happen – that Rory would get that music bug once again. Rory for his part had fought it all week but was only too keen to jump at a chance to be on stage with Marie. Carmel, aggrieved, said she'd continue shopping and would see them at the Town Hall later. Despite Oonagh's reckless driving they arrived in one piece, but late, at the venue. Oonagh dumped Rory at the door and hurtled off to Sligo General to check up on and reprimand her other bass player.

Rory took a while to warm up and a little longer to learn the bands' ways but after two run-throughs, he started to get the hang of it. He was a far better bass player than Eamonn Darcy – *Perhaps those two local girls have done us a favour,* thought Marie. The other boys in the band were a little surprised at Marie's newly revealed patience. She waited while Rory questioned the tempo, adjusted his amp and reworked some introductions and then sang all her numbers with a newly acquired gusto. It was just as well Oonagh wasn't there. She would have sussed it out straight away. Rory and Donna Marie were flirting with each other.

In the provincial A&E while Eamonn waited for his X-Ray results he felt ashamed. The ear-bashing Oonagh had given him, was worse than the pain in his throbbing hand. "Bad enough to damage a few tendons, but worse to miss out on the best gig of the season." Her sitting beside him waiting for the results only made his guilt worsen. He hadn't even had a good feel, never mind anything else and he'd invited the girls to tonight's show. What a prick. What a poor shrivelled-up woman-fearing prick.

On the drive back to the town hall Oonagh laughed to herself, more out of relief than because there was anything amusing. As was usual with Oonagh her laughter turned to concern. Had she been too tough on Eamonn? It had been an accident after all.

Well, it was too late to do anything about that now and perhaps his not being able to play for a while was punishment enough. She was surprised to see her charges in the car park of the town hall when she arrived. They were joking and laughing and it took them a while to ask after Eamonn. "He's broken his two middle fingers."

"Poor bastard," said Marie. As a performer she knew exactly how Eamonn must have been feeling. It was only that very afternoon that Marie had realised that a performer was what she always had been. She'd found the sudden line-up change a challenge, she'd found the sudden news of her husband a challenge but she'd risen to both those challenges that afternoon. For the first time in her life she felt supremely confident.

Sligo Town Hall was not an ideal venue. Built at a time of prosperity its formality made it less adaptable than many of the promoters would have liked. It did, however, have the largest seating capacity in the town – apart from St Aloysius' the biggest of the five local churches and tonight, unlike its religious counterparts, it was well filled. The bar in the reception area was doing a roaring trade and the varied programme leant itself to an eclectic mix of tourists and locals.

Donna Marie and Deep South were to open and close the gig. Marie began quietly – 'With a Song in my Heart' was one of her favourites and she started it without the band. Oonagh was nervous. Marie's voice cracked on the second line – God, would she get through the first song? For Marie, there was no adorable face to behold. Michael, whom she'd grown to adore, was elsewhere but as the band accompanied her with swelling music she found the strength to make her voice soar. Her quiet pure tone wrapped the hall drawing the listeners towards her. All divas need to experience pain – a churning deep in the gut, a longing buried in the soul that gives an extra resonance to their lives and their singing. That evening all heard it. Rory had never seen Marie so moving and so moved. Oonagh sensed that Marie's loss was Donna Marie's gain. Marie had escaped from her mother, escaped from her husband and was finding her true voice – a voice that Oonagh had longed to hear in their years' apart.

Seamlessly Marie and Deep South interwove soul with Irish traditional, jazz with country. By the final song in the first set the room vibrated with appreciation. The American duo that followed them had a difficult time. The local quartet had a better reception. As Oonagh helped Marie to change her dress and re-apply her make up for the second set the boys in the band smiled at each other – this was the best gig of all.

Eamonn Darcy, his hands still throbbing, had watched the second set from the back of the hall. He was jealous of Rory and annoyed with himself. Sexual aspirations had forced him to miss out on the greatest pleasure of all. When would Deep South ever have a crowd so 'onside' again?

From the other side of the room someone else had been watching. Every detail was being scrutinised, every blink and smile analysed. Carmel Fuscoe, having lost her baby was now losing her husband – whether to Marie Downey or to Deep South the result would be the same. Endless nights of waiting, of hoping; endless days of being second in line. Admitting defeat, she went backstage to congratulate them. It was an impressive thirty minutes. Even a deceived wife had to admit that. Carmel wanted to be excited for her husband. Learning to know when to let go was all part of an adult relationship. They'd lived in each other's pockets for far too long. What she'd just seen on stage was the happy man she'd married – the man full of hope, the man who had helped her to dream. It was time to let others share those dreams.

Eamonn was sorry he'd gone backstage. The boys taking the piss, was bad enough but most hurtful of all was their appreciation of Rory. Worse than that, was the way Oonagh and Marie ignored him. For them, he'd been unthoughtful and unprofessional. He'd let them down and as he couldn't perform he had no place backstage.

The second set, the set with which they closed the evening was more frenetic than the first. It left the crowd and the band in a state of thrilled exhaustion. Donna Marie's red silk dress was damp with effort, Rory's face was drained by concentration and Oonagh was silenced by relief. "I'm bloody starving," said Marie pulling on her leisure suit. "Let's head off and get some chips." With all the worry over Michael, the hospital visit, the concern over Marie and the excitement of the show Oonagh had forgotten to eat. She too was ravenous. Gerry the Council caretaker gave them directions to a local chippy. Carmel and Rory were nipping off to Jury's for the late licence and the boys in the band had the packing up to do. *Perfect,* thought Marie, *It's just us girls now.* They found the Four Lanterns without any bother. It was the only chip shop in the town open that late. As Marie went in to queue for two fish suppers, Oonagh reversed into a parking space and waited. It was as she was tuning the radio that it happened – she saw him – Michael Truesdale – walking out of the Horseshoe Bar and getting into a clapped out Rover. Without a first thought, let alone a second, Oonagh turned on the ignition, indicated right and began to follow the car. She'd seen Cagney and Lacey. She'd watched episodes of Columbo and she still had no idea what she was doing. What if he saw her? What would she do if he stopped his car? Was this not just madness? All these questions jumbled in her head as she gear changed and braked from corner to corner. With the car seat damp with nerves and her eyes wide with fear Oonagh concentrated on both the road and her driving. Minutes felt like hours as they headed out of Sligo town along past the mud-filled drug addict filled swimming pool and out into the open country. Well it was open country to Oonagh. To anyone else it was town outskirts.

As abruptly as he'd appeared Michael Truesdale parked in a narrow street, walked down a short pathway and entered a small semi-detached house. Oonagh drove on, parked on a corner and sat in the car breathing heavily. She fumbled in her handbag for a scrap of paper and a chewed biro. Where was that bloody Filofax when you needed it! Still panting she got out of the car, scribbled a note of the street name and walked back towards the house. She couldn't see a number but the name on the gate said 'West ways' and that would just have to do. Like the shorthaired one who is married to Harvey, she ran back to the car and retraced her route all the way to the Four Lanterns.

"Where the fuck have you been? I've been standing here like a local whore for ages – and your chips are cold." Oonagh didn't feel like chips. Her stomach was churning. "I'm so sorry Marie but I think I've seen him."

"What?"

"Michael, I think I've seen him. I've written down the address. I didn't know what else to do." Marie couldn't offer any advice. The fish she'd eaten repeated on her. The news made her doubly sick. What the hell was going on?

For both women the night was long. Oonagh's initial panic, now shared and overtaken by Marie's, increased hourly. There was no way she could retrace her route in the dark. It would take those hours. This much-parried suggestion exhausted itself by four thirty. They still had no idea of what was to be done. Oonagh had only caught a glimpse of the man she thought was Michael – what if she'd followed a complete stranger? If it happened to Cagney and Lacey it could surely happen to her. On several occasions after the bombing she'd been accosted in the street by people she didn't recognise. She'd later approached one of them in a shop queue only to discover it wasn't the person she thought. That evening she'd driven off in a state of blind panic – what if the blindness was a reality?

They'd let themselves into Theresa Coyne's. She always had a key under the left hand geranium – a description she gave even when geraniums were out of season. Their whispered debates that started in the garden lingered on till dawn. They didn't sleep all night. Marie was convinced and unconvinced that Michael was in Sligo. When convinced she wondered what he was doing there, why he hadn't made contact. When unconvinced, Oonagh was suffering from exhaustion. All the pressure had simply been too much for her still grieving friend.

Theresa Coyne was in fine fettle over breakfast. She hadn't heard the girls get in but news of the Town hall gig had reached her and she congratulated both 'agent and star' by opening a fresh jar of homemade damson jam. The girls had little appetite and although the gesture was much appreciated the proud produce remained untouched. "Bit of a night was it?" smiled Theresa as she cleared away the uneaten cold cooked breakfasts. "Yes, yes it was," replied Oonagh, regretting the waste of food and their uncustomary unkindness to the host. They waited for what little breakfast they'd had to take effect and then asked Mrs Coyne if they could put them up for another night. She was thrilled, the damson jam must have done the trick after all and she didn't need that room until Sunday night with the Teakles arrived. She liked the Teakles – two teachers from Belfast. They always came down just after the festival – he wasn't one for music, or so Attracta the wife had told her. At the time Theresa had thought that a great shame and over the past six years her opinion hadn't altered.

The indecisive couple, Oonagh and Marie, sat on the garden seat outside their lodgings and wondered what to do. The 'what ifs' were endless and merely confused them, "Well," concluded Marie, "It's better to know if you are right or not so for God's sake let's take a run out there and have a look." She took the car keys from her friend. "I'll drive. That way you'll be able to look out for signs and to show me just where you think this bastard is." This seemed like a decent plan but like all their plans the execution wasn't easy. Daylight transforms things; it gives hope to the hopeless and exposes the dying. For Oonagh, who'd once needed its warm hope the daylight was damning. It revealed possibilities she hadn't seen the night before; a quaint set of bungalows here, a new crossroads there, and too many left and right turns for her to be convinced of anything. If ever she needed divine guidance it was now. She couldn't be wrong. She must have seen Michael. She had followed him to his door. She must be able to retrace her route. After the third wrong right turning Marie pulled the car into the side of the road, turned off the ignition, slumped over the wheel and began to cry. "This is stupid Oonagh, bloody stupid. We'll never find him and if we do it probably won't be him anyway." Oonagh said nothing. With her hands pressed hard into the vinyl seats, she prayed to St Anthony, surely he could help them find the lost husband? She prayed to her boys, surely they could guide her; they'd both always looked out for her in the past. She prayed to God, the God who had taken them from her. Somehow, as she released her angry grip she found the strength within to comfort Marie and to spur her on. "Let's just try turning right a little further up the road. I'm sure we're not very far away now." Her friend was years away; wondering where her future had gone, wondering if she could have foreseen this present, "Com'on Marie. If I'm wrong this time we'll drive to Ross' Point and spend the afternoon getting a wee bit of colour."

"Christ Oonagh, you sound just like my mother. I suppose you've got some Johnson's baby oil in that bag of yours." Oonagh hadn't. She'd left it on the bed of the B&B but she laughed none the less. In that laughter, like so many of Ulster's inhabitants, they found the strength to continue.

The house Oonagh pointed out was unassuming, not at all the kind of place Michael would have chosen. Oonagh thought it might be a Bed and Breakfast but there were no outward signs of business, no ratings' board or panel advertising vacancies. Now they'd found the house neither Marie nor Oonagh had a clue what to do next. "Let's just think for a minute," Marie had done nothing but think. At every gig she'd been sure Michael had been watching her, checking up on her as he always did. He wouldn't have liked her on stage flirting with Rory. He'd have hated the mixture of styles and he'd not be at all keen on Oonagh representing the agency. Marie had said nothing of these fears or judgements to her friend. Oonagh would have just called it nonsense – her word for neurosis, paranoia or anything that prevented someone achieving. Ironically Oonagh was full of 'nonsenses' and although the trip had made her more assured she was bound to return to that uncertain Oonagh when they got back to Belfast. "Well Marie. You've been thinking for at least half an hour now and we can't just sit here. Do you want me to go to the door and ask for him?"

"No, no Oonagh I'll do it. Just give me a minute." They sat on in the car. Marie was too worried to budge. By meeting Michael she'd learn the truth about their relationship; the truth about the last ten years. The trappings of success they had had, but her lack of offspring and her non-performing had made those years pointless. She wasn't sure she'd ever known the real Michael – until last night on stage she hadn't ever known the real her – and now she was being forced to confront that knowledge, to admit her life had been a sham and worse still, to consider that her mother with her West Belfast snobbery and her entrenched views was right all along. Even if the truth is hurtful at least you know where you stand. "Right Oonagh, com'on."

They walked through the gate and up the dull cement path to the door. Marie rang the doorbell. She couldn't hear it resonate round the hall. She rang it again forcefully. *God, I'm so like my mother,* Oonagh thought exactly that but neither friend communicated the thought. "You'd better knock. That bell's not working." Michael couldn't possibly be there. Michael couldn't possibly sleep in a house where so many things needed doing. Twice more Marie knocked, but there was no answer. "Com'on. Let's head off to Ross' Point and catch those rays." Somewhat disappointed Oonagh acknowledged Marie's suggestion and they turned from the door.

"Hello. Can I help you?"

A red headed woman with a curious toddler was at the gate. She walked towards them smiling. "Michael, I'll let you off the reigns if you stay on the grass." She unleashed the boy who wobbled on the dry lawn for a few seconds before falling onto his bottom to stare at the strangers. "We're down here on a wee trip from Belfast and we were hoping to catch up with our old mate Michael." Oonagh amazed herself.

"Oh Christ knows where he is. Now that the Festival has finished he's probably having a few jars with the bands. He'll be back in time to put himself to bed at about half past five. Why don't you call around about six? Shall I tell him you called?"

"No, no," uttered Marie. "We want to surprise him."

"Michael don't eat that, it's dirty. Sorry I'll have to go before he demolishes the whole garden."

Oonagh walked Marie down the path – their legs were slow but their minds were racing. They said nothing on the road to Ross' Point. They said nothing as they took the car rug from the boot and spread it on the sand dunes. Oonagh was the first to break the silence.

"It won't be Michael – sure he hates children. I've made a mistake Marie."

"But there is someone called Michael in that house."

"It's a coincidence I'm sure. Besides he's called Micheal and there's no way a Truesdale would give himself over to the Gaelic."

Marie thought of the boy in the dirt. He looked nothing like her husband – sure his hair was the same colour but everyone was mucky brown at that age. No – her Michael was in Dublin building up a business – he'd be back to her when he had sorted things out. Oonagh got them two chips from the burger van in the car park and the two worriers sat worrying out to sea.

For Oonagh, the excited panic of last night's chase had disappeared but she still felt nervous about her revelation. What if, as Marie believed, it wasn't Michael after all? How ridiculous would she look? Oonagh had often been made to look ridiculous. She'd been tied to a lamppost outside the hairdresser's and covered with Ambrosia creamed rice and toilet rolls on the weekend before her wedding. Sean had helped to preserve her dignity and had seen her safely dead. There was no Sean to help her now and this time she had given herself totally to the situation. She'd followed the car, abandoning Marie outside the chippy. Then she had been so sure. Yet she wasn't so sure now – perhaps she should have left well alone. Marie had needed to find answers, even if she seldom said that, and Oonagh knew that the not knowing was killing her. Secretly Marie was mourning the loss of her husband and the death of her marriage. Like Oonagh at her family funeral she was putting a brave face on it, but at least Oonagh had kissed the coffined boys goodbye. Marie had so far been denied that chance. As she ate salty chips Oonagh thought of herself as lucky. She'd been able to lay her boys to rest even if that meant daily turmoil for her. Many in Ireland would never rediscover their loved ones; they'd disappeared without trace, their whereabouts unknown. The forests of Ireland were peopled with such anonymity. What if Michael were one of those? What if Rory was wrong? What if they were thinking ill of the dead?

Marie stared at the waves and tasted their salt. What if Oonagh was wrong? She'd not have said it out of spite – Oonagh would never do that – she always told the truth. But what if she'd wanted to see someone so much that, for her friend's sake, she'd convinced herself that she had? The woman at the gate must think them a pair of idiots – wait 'til they returned to the house to discover that the man they'd labelled 'their mate' was a total stranger. Choking on a cold chip Marie laughed at the ridiculousness of the situation. They should have stuck to their plan and returned to Belfast. Michael Truesdale was known for his straight talking – if he had wanted to leave her why hadn't he just said so. No, she and Oonagh had been doing him a great disservice. He may have a Dublin office but he could still have been abducted. She rolled up the greasy paper and walked to the greasy bin. It smelled of summer excesses so Marie stood well back to propel her rubbish. Three attempts it took – Oonagh's laughter put her off, or so she claimed. Oonagh landed the rubbish in two. A teenager looked at the two women. "Youse two are mad," he said scraping his bike along the pavement. "He's no fool," laughed Marie as she folded the car rug, and they returned to Beaupre.

While Oonagh struggled with Mrs Coyne's middle of the range-pressurised shower, Marie telephoned her mother from the lounge to announce their changed plans.

"We'll be back tomorrow."

"In time for lunch?" asked Moira Downey, annoyed that she hadn't bought enough pork fillet.

"No, it will probably be late afternoon, depending…"

"Depending on what exactly?" asked Moira Downey. Her hatred of unfinished sentences all too apparent in her tone.

"Well, we've got to check up on someone before we leave."

She couldn't tell her mother what was going on. It would just be another example of 'Marie going off the rails'.

"Oh, have you heard from that bloody husband of yours? It's a disgrace the way he is behaving; I've a good mind to…"

Marie let her mother drone on the way she always had. In silence she waited for the familiar and tell-tale signs to appear – the falling intonation that so often led to 'another thing'. This time it was followed by an oddly caring, "Are you alright Marie?" Fearful that, yet again, she had overstepped the mark Moira Downey was at last trying to show a little concern for her daughter's wellbeing.

"I'm fine mum. Listen I have to go the shower's free. Thank Dad for looking after the house and we'll see you soon."

"Bye now and look after yourself."

Marie put some coins in the telephone box and noted the duration of the call. It was Mrs Coyne's home telephone and she always made sure that although permission was granted for its use she'd never be out of pocket. Theresa Coyne emptied the wooden telephone box every evening to check that the noted durations matched the donations.

Marie showered away call and beach residue and applied an extra layer of body lotion to her reddened skin. She took special care with this – if she was to be meeting Michael again she needed to be looking her best. Oonagh had applied an extra splash of cologne and her favourite pale blue outfit. Together they shone like fresh colours on a paint chart – even Theresa commented how 'grand' they looked. Marie took the wheel. Oonagh didn't mind as her white sling-backs weren't good for driving. She'd ruined several pairs of heels that way without thinking. They took their time on the drive to 'Westways,' planning to get there just as the wee lad was asleep. Parking up at six o'clock they both checked hair and make-up and walked down the grey path to the front door.

"Come in, come in… Michael's not here yet so I've put the baby to bed. He shouldn't be long now. Have a seat in the back room and I'll get us all a wee cup of tea." The woman rubbed her stomach in a way all too familiar to one of the visitors.

"Would you like me to give you a hand?" enquired Oonagh.

"No, no, I'll manage. I'm alright for a fair few months yet."

Reassured by her instincts Oonagh followed Marie into the sitting room. Marie was blood-blotched – her forehead lined with anger. In her hands a gilded frame; a picture of Michael and the woman who was now making tea. To anyone else it would have been a carefree picture but to the visitors it was an image of betrayal. Her cream two-piece suit, his grey flannel jacket, the virginal bouquet, the confetti blowing round the church porch; There was no mistaking this was a wedding day picture. Oonagh was flustered. Had Michael been married before and not told her friend? Had he married since and not told the householder? Was the woman in the picture his sister? Had he been giving a friend away? With confusion such as this Oonagh slumped onto the velveteen sofa beside her friend and placed the picture on the side table where it had resided.

"I've brought a few Jaffa Cakes to go with the tea – sorry. We do the weekly shop on Monday."

Marie wondered who the 'we' was. Was this pregnant woman talking about her husband? Was the child in her belly, his? She put the cup and saucer on her lap to stop it shaking.

"So – how do you know Michael?"

Marie couldn't speak. All the things she wanted to say were too brutal. She was no good at catfights. The woman asking the questions was just like herself in the early days – full of hope. Oonagh jumped in.

"Oh we used to be in the same business – that's why we are down, for the festival. Donna Marie has been doing a few gigs."

"Yes, yes… that's right," said Marie.

"We were at the Town Hall last night."

"Jesus, it's a small world – I'm surprised you didn't bump into Michael there. The Delaney's, one of his acts was playing there too."

So, Marie had been right all along. He had been watching her all the time. What must he be thinking? There was no way he'd come back to her now.

"The Delaney's?" asked Oonagh.

"Yes, they are a double act supposedly from America but I'm sure the woman's got relations in Waterford."

It was typical of Michael to have pseudo-Americans on his books. It was just the type of wool pulling he admired. Oonagh didn't think they had much going for them. They were a little too 'folk singer' for her liking.

"So how did you and my..." Marie stopped herself before the noun formed. What would that noun have been – husband? Ex-husband? Fancy man? Only she knew –

"...Michael meet?"

"Oh, too long ago I was a singer – well, I did a few amateur nights round the town. I don't sing anymore. Michael and the house keep me busy enough especially as he's away a lot in Dublin or in the north."

Marie looked at Oonagh. Oonagh looked at Marie. This story sounded all too familiar. Had Michael killed this woman's dreams as he had Marie's? The cup in Marie's lap upturned.

"Oh dear, I'll get a damp cloth." Marie's fresher mirror image went into the kitchen.

"What the fuck is going on here? What the fuck do we do now?"

Although all too aware of what might be going on, Oonagh could neither share this with her friend and had no answer to either of her questions.

"There we go," Geraldine handed over the cloth and went to take the cup and saucer. Marie grabbed hold of her hand, the grip a little too tight, and the speed of the attack a little too obvious.

"And do you love him, do you?"

Geraldine, taken aback by the question, replied forcefully, "Oh yes, he's the only man for me."

The telephone in the hall prevented further assaults. Oonagh tried to calm her friend by holding fast to her shaking wrist.

"Right, I'll tell them... and drive safely." Geraldine returned to the sitting room.

"That was Michael; he's had to go to Dublin at short notice. He won't be back 'til Tuesday at the earliest."

"Well, that's too long a wait even for us," smiled Oonagh.

"We'd best be off – thanks for the tea." Marie also stood up to go.

"You've a lovely home and a lovely family – look after them."

"Oh I shall," said Geraldine. "I shall." She waved at them from the door. Marie crumbled when they got into the car. None of this, none of it made any sense. She was drained. Oonagh drove back to Mrs Coyne's, barefoot and helped Marie to bed. Theresa noted their distress and brewed a comforting cup of tea. By the second pot, Oonagh had told their story.

Chapter Fourteen

Michael Dale was late at the town hall that Friday. The first act was on when he arrived; the first act which took his breath away, prevented him from going backstage to wish the Delaney's luck and made him feel like a coward. This Donna Marie was his wife – strutting around on stage flirting with both audience and bass player. She looked like an independent woman. She didn't need him. He had done the right thing by leaving her. Besides, he had grown tired of the travelling, tired of being always on the road. He hated always having to have some clothes in the dry-cleaners. Sure Marie had wanted children but four kids and another on the way was enough for anyone's husband. Belfast had been a good base for him but now, as the troubles seemed to be easing off and more people were going across the border his money-making schemes and his different lives were likely to be discovered. Geraldine's latest bit of emotional blackmail, getting herself pregnant was the last straw. He'd have to sever his ties with the north but couldn't do that cleanly.

Michael had fretted about this for weeks. He'd moved some of his clients to the Dublin office – not too many as Marie would have grown suspicious. He'd picked the day of departure. It was a bit dramatic but the decision was based on the year-end and not on his emotional ties with Marie. Oonagh's presence over the past few years had reassured him – Marie wouldn't be totally on her own. That bitch of a mother who had never liked him would be of no use to anyone. No, Marie's sad little friend would help her sort things out.

The plan was to fake his own suicide, to abandon his car in Ballycastle. He'd written the note the previous day but the tenth wedding anniversary party had thrown him. He couldn't bring himself to totally break Marie's heart. He'd driven round and round wondering what to do and eventually left the car in a

Dunmurry side street. It was late and his bag was heavy. He took a room at the Dunmurry Lodge signing in as Michael Dale and drank the mini bar dry. The following morning he bussed to Central Station and took the train to Dublin. While he showered she cooked him some breakfast. She was a great girl. They'd been lovers for years. She never wanted to meet Marie – singing was her life and shagging her manager was a bonus. Orla never minded being 'the bit on the side'. That wife who thought herself a performer was a stuck up bitch. Now that Orla had transferred her talents to the Dublin agency there was no need to deal with Marie Truesdale. Sure she'd had to lie and say she was giving up the business. It was a half-truth. Donna was no more and Orla could be her real name on stage and off. Michael spent the whole weekend in the pokey flat off Leeson Street. Orla was great in the kitchen and bed. He enjoyed the guilt free eating and the guilt free sex. She never talked about the business nor asked him where he'd been. She accepted the newness of everything. Orla had no option; the results from the clinic had not been good. She had six months – why shouldn't she enjoy them?

Theresa Coyne was not only a great guesthouse proprietor, she was also at the centre of the community – "Why didn't you tell me earlier? Sure I know everyone in this town and if I don't they are not worth knowing."

Marie walked into the kitchen – she looked terrible.

"Oonagh was just telling me about your troubles. Sure men are all the same. They cannot be trusted. You sit yourself down there in Martin's chair – he's not here so it's no use to him – and I'll get you a little something to steady your nerves."

Marie did just as she was told and Theresa went into the front room for the brandy.

"I'm sorry Marie. It just came out…"

"Och Oonagh, I'm glad you told her. She might help us find the bastard. I just want to know the truth. I just want to get to the bottom of this once and for all."

"Now," said Theresa, pouring herself a half'un. "I'll move you into one of the family rooms for a few days. There will be no charge for that. Call it helping out a couple of friends in need. Sure Monday's time to be heading back to Belfast with all these shenanigans."

"What's the point of staying in Sligo while he's in Dublin?" asked Marie.

"And what are you going to do? Tear up and down Grafton Street until you find him? No... you girls need a few days rest and a few local leads before heading back to Belfast. Sure, haven't you a business to run?" Theresa was shrewd. They did need to think of the long term as well as the short.

"Now, there's the phone. Call whoever you have to and what do you say we pop up to Jury's for our tea?" Theresa Coyne had become part of a detective squad. She could furnish them with local knowledge, at a price; that price was their friendship for, with the girls gone and her husband always away at the golf, Theresa was lonely. Oonagh called her parents. She was ten and a half again.

"Are youse enjoying yourselves, love? What's the weather been like?"

"Ma, we spotted Michael... Michael Truesdale..."

"Hold on, I'll get your Da."

Quite what Oonagh's father would do is to remain a mystery for in times of need her mother always passed over the phone. Oonagh's father listened and only said,

"Poor wee Marie," when the story was concluded.

"Don't be doing anything daft now Oonagh – if a man doesn't want to be found he won't."

"But Da, Marie needs some answers."

"And you really think that finding him will give you answers? What if some things are better left unanswered? You just look after yourself."

"Sure Da, see you on Monday."

Marie's call was more difficult.

"So, have you finally decided when you are coming back? Did you see anything in the shops?" It was typical that Moira Downey heard nothing in her child's voice. She sensed none of her pain, none of the worry, none of the distance between them. She was affronted when Marie asked, "Is Dad there?" They'd always tried to exclude her, those two. After all she'd done for them they still made her feel like an outsider.

"I'll just get him for you, hold the line."

Marie knew her mother was angry but didn't really care. There was no way Moira Downey would have listened to what she had to say without comment and comment was the last thing Marie needed.

"I think you two should come home Marie. You'll only get hurt. Dashing off to Dublin on a wild goose chase is not the answer." Marie laughed. Michael may be many things but a wild goose chase he certainly was not.

"Dad, we'll have a couple of more days here and we'll be back in Belfast on Monday."

"Besides, you don't know what kind of crowd he's mixed up with."

"I think I have a fair idea."

"Alright, look after yourselves – do you want to say goodbye to your mother?"

A steely voiced Moira Downey wished her daughter well – it didn't make either of them feel any better.

Chapter Fifteen

Life for Brid Armstrong was hard enough. The flat off Kilburn High Road was too small for herself and the boys – especially as they were growing into men. Her thirteen-year-old twins were her pride and joy. They looked a lot like their father but that hadn't put her off. Michael Armstrong was a philanderer. She'd known that from the first day she'd set eyes on him at the fleadh. He was playing the drums with an Anglo-Irish five piece that looked a little out of place at this annual celebration of republican music. At the open-air bar he had made a beeline for her – or so he had said. He was over for the fortnight and wondered if he could take her out for a bite to eat. No one ever asked Brid out so she jumped at the chance. Six months later, while he was off on one of his gigs she found herself pregnant. There was no doubt in her mind that he was the father but he took a bit of persuading. They married in a pokey registry office. Only her best friend, Imelda who worked in the off-licence came to see them tie the knot. Two strangers acted as last minute witnesses. She'd thought it odd that none of his family wanted to know her – especially after the twins were born. The boys were beautiful – mini images of their father and for the first year of their lives all went well. Michael was away a lot but Imelda gave her a hand when she needed it. Imelda wasn't able to have children – she had problems with her tubes so they had often joked that the boys were half hers. It was a cruel blow that she lost her best friend and her husband on the same day.

It was the afternoon of the boys' first birthday. Imelda had come round on her day off to ice the cake. The flat was cramped so Brid had decided to take the boys out in the pram for a breath of fresh air so Imelda could get on with it. If only she had known that Michael was coming back for the boys she'd not have left. Grey clouds and thin rain curtailed her trip and fearful of the twins catching a cold she returned to the flat. If only she hadn't. If only the boys hadn't fallen asleep in the pram. If only they'd have heard and been heard.

She smelled him before she saw him. There was no mistaking the Paco Rabanne. She'd bought it for him at Christmas and he kept it for special occasions. What was so special about him fucking her best friend against the sink? Brid stood in the doorway. She watched as her husband, the father of her children, pounded away at Imelda. He'd never said he liked her. How ridiculous they looked. At least they were on the third floor so none of the neighbours would know. Brid waited until they'd finished – it wasn't long. She knew the signs.

"How's the cake doing?" she asked

There was no going back now. She told her friend to leave. She told her husband to leave. She celebrated her boys' birthday with a few balloons and a shop bought Madeira. It was the first of many birthdays they'd share alone.

Michael felt awful. He'd thought that Brid was baking something in the kitchen. He'd been too excited by the notion to consider the change in personnel. All women to him were an opportunity and this was an opportunity he'd had to take. Imelda hadn't said no. She didn't have a regular boyfriend and her voracious sexual appetite had put a lot of men off. She was just too needy.

Often he tried to see the boys. Brid allowed him to send them presents at Christmas and on their birthdays but when he called round it was always 'inconvenient'. Besides, it wasn't easy getting back from Belfast or Dublin. His three monthly visits became six monthly and then not at all. He sent a registered letter with money every month and then extra notes at Christmas. This didn't ever stop. Sometimes it was a Belfast postmark, sometimes Dublin and occasionally Sligo.

"Your father certainly gets around," she'd say to the boys. None of them really knew how true that was.

He'd had nowhere to go when she chucked him out. One of the boys in the original band – Eamonn Truesdale had started up a small talent agency in Belfast. He suggested that Michael came over for a few weeks to see how it went. It went well. Eamonn showed him what he knew but Michael was a natural – he could charm the birds off the trees and the knickers off your best friend.

Eamonn Truesdale was older than Michael and had less ambition. They were like father and son and it was only natural that, after the heart attack Truesdale talent should be left to him. Michael always had the goodwill – now he had the business. At Eamonn's funeral he was treated like a son, it was only fitting that he should behave as one.

Chapter Sixteen

Theresa Coyne loved Miss Marple and although there was no body as yet, she rustled up a few local experts who might be able to track down the suspect. For Theresa the crime was like a murder. This man, this Michael Truesdale, had obviously abandoned his lovely talented wife for some young bit of skirt. To Theresa, marriage was sacred; its vows were never to be broken. Whatever the problems, they had to be worked through. God knows, she'd done enough 'working through' with Martin to become an expert. By the time the trio arrived in Jury's for that wee drink, Theresa had assembled both knowledgeable and sympathetic ears.

"I hope you don't mind but I've let a few friends in on our secret."

Marie could see they were all sympathetic – the nodding heads and watery eyes showed that but six people were too much. Oonagh and Marie were pleased to see Kieran O'Donoghue – he had helped them out once and perhaps he would do so again.

"I told you you'd be fine with Theresa," he said, introducing his wife – a warm portly woman with a flushed face and a firm handshake.

"What will you have to drink?" she asked, forcing her husband to put his hand in his pocket for once. It was quite a big round but they could afford it.

So there they were; the alternative Sligo CID, the O'Donoghues, Theresa Coyne, Father Ignatius and his housekeeper Aiofe, Pat O'Flaherty and a large woman who worked as secretary for Sligo Feis. Marie and Oonagh didn't catch her name. She had such a little voice for such a large woman.

"So," said Theresa, sipping her brandy and ginger and calling the meeting, for that's what she considered it, to order. "Tell us exactly what happened."

Jointly Oonagh and Marie told of the car pursuit, the discovery of the house, the other woman revelation and the still missing husband. Aoife thought she knew the wee girl –

"You know, I think that's the young O'Flaherty girl, the one that used to sing in the choir at the Holy Cross. She had a lovely voice, there was talk of her taking it up professionally but then she met some Englishman. Her mother wasn't at all pleased. They all stopped coming to Mass. Don't you remember, Father?"

Father Ignatius did indeed remember. The shame of that baby had almost killed Mrs O'Flaherty.

"I tried to visit a few times but there was never anyone in. They didn't get married with us. I suspect they went to Dublin."

"But he can't be married to her – he's been married to me for ten bloody years."

Theresa Coyne drained her glass.

"Well, it's a matter for the Gards. You'll need to report it in Belfast and we'll see Sergeant Morrow at Mass tomorrow. He'll know what to do here. Call that waiter over, Dervla. We need something to steady our nerves."

The Feis' secretary summoned a lank adolescent and ordered the same again. They'd just paid for the drinks when Rory and Carmel arrived in. Oonagh and Marie were pleased to see them. The way things were going you'd have thought this was Theresa Coyne's problem. Rory grabbed an extra seat and Carmel bunched up beside Marie. Oonagh, in whispered tones filled them in on what had happened.

"Have you spoken with your Dad?" asked Rory

"Well, sort of…"

"He'll have to get you a good solicitor – we can do that on Monday. There's nothing much more you can do now."

"You should tell that to her," whispered Oonagh, nodding at Theresa. She was going over every detail, the constant tuts and sympathetic gazes at Marie, her all too obvious punctuation. The Belfast four had had enough –

"I'll just walk the girls back to the house," said Rory taking control of the situation.

"I'll come with you," said Carmel, glad of an escape route lest she herself should come under scrutiny.

"See you in the morning girls – we'll go to the ten o'clock."

With a smiled goodnight they left the Sligo Seven to pour over Marie's marriage and to sympathise with a poor wee local girl who had been duped by an English protestant.

"Why don't we spend the day together tomorrow?" suggested Carmel, as they arrived at the door of Beaupre. She knew what it was like to be in a state and a ranting Irish woman was not what Marie needed.

"But what about Mass?"

"Forget Mass. Besides, do you really want all and sundry knowing your business?"

"She's right, Marie," added Oonagh. "Let's try to just have one day away from it all before we go back to Belfast."

"Ok."

"Right, we'll pick you up at nine – come on Carmel, you need your beauty sleep!"

"You cheeky bastard," laughed Marie.

"We'll see you at nine."

With that Carmel and Rory walked back to Jury's to collect their car. They'd no idea what they were to do tomorrow. They just felt sorry for a good woman who had been betrayed.

It was quiet in the Coynes that night. Oonagh and Marie could hear themselves think – it was good that they couldn't hear each other. Marie was too upset to speak. The man she'd married, the man who'd convinced her not to have children, had fathered children and married someone else. Geraldine was pretty, but no prettier than her ten years ago. How could either of them have fallen for his deception? Marie thought Geraldine as stupid as herself. All those trips away. All those ill matched new clothes. How could Michael have been so cruel to her? Obviously he had kept up the facade for at least three years so why had their tenth anniversary forced him to leave?

Oonagh felt so, so sorry for Geraldine. Her life would be torn apart. Her children would be left without a father. Her marriage would be labelled a sham. Marie had been betrayed, but Marie could cope. She was, as any family doctor would say, "Well on the way to recovery." But that poor wee girl, in that poor wee house would be devastated. Oonagh and she had so much in common. Yet there was no Marie with a big house and a warm heart to help her. Oonagh knew what it was like to feel so completely alone – Geraldine would have all that to come.

Carmel, in the Murphy's spare room with Rory at her side, felt sorry for both Marie and Geraldine. They'd both been duped by an unworthy man. At least in Rory she'd found honesty even if it sometimes pained her. He only ever lied for her sake and for that she was truly grateful.

Chapter Seventeen

Theresa was a little put out. She had planned to take the girls to ten o'clock mass, speak with Kieran Morrow and track down the two-timing shite but those women, despite her having put herself out for them were having none of it.

"I think it's better if I let the RUC know first. They might be able to find Michael quicker. After all he's lived longer in Belfast than he has in Sligo."

Marie was his wife, or one of them, so Theresa felt obliged to accept her wishes.

"It's probably best if we keep a lid on things," said Oonagh, "for now at least."

Theresa had often been told to keep things a secret – it seldom worked. She was behind with their breakfasts. It was her own fault for getting up so early. Her annoyance over the breakfast and at being told to keep her mouth shut showed in her blotchy neck and her trembling hand. She almost scalded Oonagh with the tea.

Carmel and Rory arrived at nine o'clock on the dot. Kieran O'Shaunessey had lent them his estate car and although there was a slight smell of dog there was plenty of room. Theresa told them to 'have a nice day' but she wasn't sure if such a thing was possible if you skipped Mass. Over breakfast, Carmel and Rory had wondered where to take the girls. Ben Bulben Head, Innishfree and Galway had all been considered.

"We all need a bit of a laugh and none of those places seem that jolly to me."

"Och Carmel, what about a wee trip to Bundoran?"

It was a perfect suggestion and coming from a Sligo man seemed all the more acceptable.

The sunshine that had warmed them outside Beaupre faded, as they got closer to the seaside town. Bundoran, beautiful in the fifties, had faded with the years but the beach was relatively unchanged. The three women couldn't wait to ditch tights and shoes and hurtle into the sea. Rory was a little more cautious and while the girly trio teetered on the edge of the waves he manfully and single-handedly erected a much-needed windbreak. Carmel had borrowed it, a rug and some deckchairs from the O'Shaunesseys and soon a little shelter from the emotional storm was erected. She'd also blagged a flask of tea that was much welcomed after their paddle. All four of them sat sipping sweet tea and bracing themselves against the cold sea air. No matter what heat the sun manages to generate the Atlantic wind always seems to cut through it. Marie and Oonagh found the wind refreshing. So what if their hair was blown all about, so what if their arms were covered in goose pimples, they both needed to blow that week's cobwebs away. They both needed to make a fresh start on Monday.

No matter what time of day, the sea air makes you peckish and it wasn't long before Rory and Carmel set off in pursuit of hot fish and chips. Carmel took the flask with her hoping that she could charm a refill from someone. The girls had offered to go with them but someone had to mind the den.

Besides, thought Rory, *it'll give them some time to themselves.* He'd said however,

"No, no, you stay there and take in the sights."

There were sights indeed to take in. A family of four attempting to build a sandcastle. Two freckled boys playing football and an old codger walking a mangy old dog.

"Isn't this great?" remarked Oonagh. "You'd think we hadn't a care in the world."

"If only that were true – Och Oonagh, what are we going to do?"

Oonagh was glad once again to be included in Marie's plans. James Downey would help them sort things out.

"Well, we should head back to Belfast in the morning and get your dad round on his own, after lunch."

Moira Downey would only be a hindrance – they both acknowledged that.

"And then we'll get those new acts to make us both rich."

"You're right Oonagh and you need to be completely involved with the business – perhaps dad could help us set up a new company. We could make Downey Enterprises official."

Oonagh thought it strange that already Marie was excluding Michael. By having children with another woman he had excluded himself. Marie still wanted to know why he had left her and what other lies remained undiscovered, but that could wait. Right now, sitting on the windswept strand, she realised that she couldn't have survived the week without Oonagh and she wished to acknowledge that permanently.

Carmel and Rory ran along the sand. They had fish and chips for all and a fresh flask of tea. Miraculously the food was still hot, greasy and delicious. Marie collected their rubbish and walked off to the bin near the car.

"Is she really alright Oonagh?"

"I think she'll be fine. I'm just worried there's a lot more we don't know about that bastard."

"I never liked him," said Rory. "He was always crafty."

"He was always nice enough to me. He helped with all Sean's paperwork but I can't believe he has a son after all that bollocks he fed Marie."

"Well, It'll all come to light soon enough – what goes around comes around."

"Oh I do hope so Carmel," breathed Oonagh. "I do hope so."

When Marie trekked back from the bin, they sat on for a while to allow the chips to go down. Then they packed up their seaside shelter and headed for the amusements. Marie was nearly sick on the dodgems. Oonagh won a pink elephant on the shooting range; imagining every sitting duck was Michael Truesdale had helped her aim and Rory bought them all pink candyfloss. They'd shoved it at each other's mouths as they walked along the promenade, laughing at the jaded souvenirs. As kids they'd have loved those rustic egg timers and rocking-chaired leprechauns but life had removed their love of the naïve.

"Bloody hell, would you look at the price of that?" Marie stood beside a porcelain doll sat at a spinning wheel – it was thirty-eight punts.

"A bloody rip-off," said Rory, ignoring its traditional craft label. "Soon every pub in Ireland will be full of that shite." It was true that the Irish pub was taking over, but it was a packaged

Irishness sold abroad by Englishmen called Shaun. Pubs with a theme but no soul were springing up everywhere. Windows full of bootees, pictures of the potato famine, griddles and shillelaghs were being resold to the Irish. There was one such pub in Sligo's Main Street and the locals now believed it to be genuine. God, that English Shaun was a clever bastard. Cynical but invigorated they drove back to Sligo.

"Fancy a wee drink at McGlynn's before I drop you back with the old doll?"

Two rounds later they pitched up at Mrs Coynes. The girls were in fine spirits as they clambered from the car. What, with the sea and the wind the alcohol had gone straight to their heads.

"Convoy to Belfast at ten – we'll be outside."

With that Rory and Carmel drove back to the Murphys and Oonagh and Marie stood laughing on the tarmacked drive.

Mrs Coyne was showing her new guests to the room – "Mr and Mrs Teakle, this is Marie Truesdale and Oonagh O'Dwyer." A rounded baldhead looked up from a heavy suitcase – "Marie Downey, so you are still friends with Oonagh O'Callaghan."

"Why Mr Teakle, we're better friends than ever, aren't we Oonagh?"

Oonagh smiled.

"I'm not sure that's possible but it's lovely to see you both doing so well – perhaps the four of us could have lunch tomorrow?"

Theresa Coyne was annoyed. Why did no one ever include her in their plans?

"I'm afraid that won't be possible as we are heading back to Belfast in the morning."

Theresa's annoyance grew. They had changed the plans without telling her and after she'd opened up her last pot of damson jam and given them half of Martin's brandy.

It was an awkward re-union made more awkward by the narrowness of the hall and the largeness of Sean and Attracta's suitcases. The girls were embarrassed. They'd never known what to say to Sean Teakle and 'how fat you've got' which was Oonagh's thought or 'how old and bald you are' which was Marie's didn't seem appropriate. Attracta was no Annie Slevin.

"Why don't I make us all a nice cup of tea?" said Theresa, dying to get in on the act and catch up on the gossip –

"Say, in ten minutes in the lounge?"

The girls stifled their giggles 'til they got to the bedroom.

"Well, we've done it now. We'll never be able to stay here again – changing our plans without consulting bloody Miss Marple."

"Sssh Marie, thin walls have ears," chuckled Oonagh.

"Well at least we shan't have to eat any more of that bloody awful bread – I've not farted so much in years."

"That's a relief," laughed Oonagh. "I thought there was something wrong with me."

"Poor Sean Teakle, what has happened to him? He's under the thumb you can tell."

Oonagh agreed with her friend. Over tea it became obvious just how much under the thumb he was.

"Yes, I took over as head of St Brigid's when Mrs Lavery retired. She died not long after."

"Now Attracta, that had nothing to do with you. What will the girls think?"

They all laughed; all but Attracta Teakle – she was suspicious of laughter particularly laughter at her expense.

"Poor Mrs Lavery, dead. I bet she was buried in blue Crimplene," giggled Marie.

"It was a lovely service. I've been head for four years now."

"Marble cake?" asked Theresa feeling a bit left out. Funerals were normally her strong point but this was outside her parish.

"And the choir…" asked Oonagh, "Miss Slevin's choir, is that still going?"

"Oh, we don't encourage such frivolity do we Sean?"

"No Attracta, we don't."

"Didn't you once have a fling with Miss Slevin?" asked Marie, angry at this fat woman's dismissal of art, dismissal of hope, dismissal of a childhood hero.

"No, no you're mistaken," coughed Sean.

"Aren't I right enough Oonagh?"

"Yes you are Marie," Oonagh couldn't resist. "Sure Danny Byrne told me you were the father of her baby."

Sean Teakle's face reddened.

His childless wife rushed to his defence.

"Children… what are they like? They have such vivid imaginations. If Sean had made anyone pregnant I'd have known about it."

The two friends looked at each other – how could any woman unless she was a fool and married to Sean Teakle be that certain of anything?

Chapter Eighteen

Early autumn is a difficult time; it lends itself to Celtic melancholia and an anti-depressant prescription increase. For Oonagh and Marie there was no chemical imbalance – just the gentle leaf fall that was reality. Michael Truesdale had no plans to return. Oonagh knew that. Marie needed to tell him that he had betrayed her, to ask why; to call him a bastard, but she also knew that no such opportunity would present itself. There could be no victorious face slaps and a controlled cynicism could be the only result of his disappearance.

Marie was ripped apart by the void within. Why had she been so unappealing? Why had her offspring not been a desirable option? Such questions occupied her moments alone and Oonagh found herself spending more and more time in Derryvolgie Avenue.

James Downey found his daughter a solicitor who was in the Masonic. Moira Downey, as ever, did the wrong thing. Contemplating Michael's possible suicide she considered it a sin, but a justifiable and respectable one which didn't affect her family tree, barbarian, which didn't affect her family tree. After all there were no children. Divorce was too great a sin to forgive. Marie was now adamant that divorce would be the outcome. They'd hunt him down and punish him with paperwork. She realised that money was his god so why should some other cow benefit from her years of investment. On a good day Marie was convinced of her plan of action, the rest of the time she was indecisive; indecisive except when in the office. With Marie and Oonagh at the helm Downey Enterprises began to thrive. Two new acts became four, four grew to six and Donna Marie herself had a residency on Thursday, Friday and Saturday at the Strathearn Hotel. Off duty soldiers and local camp followers flocked to it and Marie was secretly thrilled that she was adding to Holywood's unacceptance of her mother. The hotel sat at the top of the town and, for Moira Downey, the posters advertising her daughter and her band became a cancer in her midst.

Marie looked on, as her family grew divided. Her father kept his own counsel; her mother's inability to do the same lessened the frequency of her visits. Moira Downey remained entrenched of Princess Gardens. Her daughter was getting out of hand.

For several months Michael Truesdale remained elusive. Sligo approaches and visits to his Dublin office were fruitless but then, in November, a man arrived, bearing news. Michael Truesdale had made a mistake. He'd attempted to poach Troy 'the international female fantasy' while he was appearing in Dublin. Troy had played along with this and Orla, after too many cosmopolitans, had invited him back for supper.

Troy, ever grateful to Marie for supporting him when Michael wouldn't, had noted the address and it was he who brought the news that Sunday evening. The girls were delighted to see him. Rory and Carmel were round for dinner, so it was simply a matter of boiling a few more potatoes and stretching what was there. Troy downed half a glass of red wine before telling the girls why he had called. In various phone calls to the agency Troy had been aware that something wasn't right and one slow Wednesday afternoon Marie had told him what was going on.

"The bastard" had been Troy's response and Marie had been glad to have someone else 'onside'. Over the homemade minestrone starter – dark nights encouraged culinary experimentation – Troy told them how Michael and a leggy blonde had approached him after a Temple Bar gig, how there were more openings in the south and how the new agency was better placed to represent him. He told how they had plied him with cocktails, invited him for supper and organised for him to sign up with the agency on Monday. He'd had no intention of doing so and had returned to Belfast, address in hand.

Rory raised his glass 'to real friends'. All toasted Troy and each other. It was going to be a long winter. Carmel was most aware of that. Eamonn Darcy's hand had not recovered well and Rory spent more time at the Strathearn Hotel than at their bar. He was only 'helping out' and, as his happiness and their relationship were greater than ever, Carmel had decided to leave well alone.

"More chicken chasseur?" enquired Oonagh circulating a heavy tureen containing her latest experiment. Her boys liked chicken better than beef; they'd have loved this, although Declan would have put all the mushrooms to one side. Kids, God they could be difficult at times.

Marie had made a lemon syllabub for pudding. Normally she put it in individual serving dishes but that Sunday she had decided on a more casual approach and had whipped her creation into a large Tyrone crystal bowl.

Thank God, she thought as she offered Troy a second helping.

They chatted late into the night. Marie was ravenous for detail; what was the flat like? Were there pictures? Who was more attractive her or Orla? Had Michael asked after her? Troy did his best to answer. Ever the diplomat he didn't wish to offend his agent and his host. Oonagh was nervous. She knew Marie still cared for Michael despite her bravado. Oonagh sympathised with her friend but her heart also went out to the pregnant mother in Sligo who, as yet, knew nothing of her betrayal. Marie would be financially well off but now that Michael had a mistress would the mother of his children be supported or would she, like Marie, be judged surplus to requirements. Where Michael Truesdale was concerned there seemed only to be questions.

Chapter Nineteen

Marie was drowning in paperwork. Questionnaires from the solicitor, tax returns, and small business allowances – all were forms of control and yet for the first time since Michael's disappearance she was calm. Oonagh was her ballast. No matter how difficult things seemed Oonagh provided a safe haven and she had lost much more than Marie ever could. Despite the form filling they were facing another Christmas without a Truesdale sighting. The start of October saw an increase in Christmas bookings so the girls raised their fees and no one complained. This was a sure sign that political stability was returning. Two unexpected arrivals that month rocked domestic stability. It had been so long ago that Oonagh had tearfully dampened the compensation forms that both she and Marie had quite forgotten that painful day – those probing questions, the personal enquiries, the lack of respect. A cheque for £50,000 was little comfort for the loss of the boys and yet as Oonagh sat alone at the kitchen table, her tears dripping into a mug of cold tea, she knew that Declan would have wanted her to look after herself. She put the cheque in her good handbag, emptied the cup into the sink and, having made sure that everything was in order boarded the bus to Marie's. The post office had brought Marie little comfort. She was still in her dressing gown when Oonagh arrived. At nine o'clock in the morning that was so unlike her.

"Look what the bastard has done now?" Marie held a letter from the Customs. The Agency that she and Michael had run was under investigation. There were five years of missing returns. No matter how they had tried to banish thoughts of Michael Truesdale, one way or another he kept reminding them of their past.

"It's about time that bloody solicitor started earning his money," said Oonagh. "Let's add this to his to-do list. We'll have a chat with him this morning and we'll get that accountant round. Together they can help sort out this mess. We've got to protect Downey Enterprises."

This morning Oonagh was fiery and it was just what Marie needed.

"Another brew?" Marie nodded; her friend obviously wanted some advice. As she poured the tea Oonagh said nothing. Once the sugar was in she rummaged in her handbag ad handed Marie an envelope.

"Go on… open it." Tentatively, Marie unveiled the cheque.

"What will you do with it?" she asked furtively.

"Well… I've had time to dwell on it, too much time really, and I think I know what's right so… I'd like to invest in us, in our future. It's going to be hard but it's time to move on. I've decided to sell the house." Although she'd been dropping hints for the last few years Marie was stunned. Oonagh only slept there two nights a week and with the boys gone it was a house not a home.

"And you'll move in here?" she asked with nervous excitement.

"I think so… but there'll be a few conditions. I want to pay my way. You've been looking after me for far too long and taking nothing in return. So I am booking us a holiday after Christmas, my treat. And then when I move in we'll half all the bills. Oh… and I want to put half of Declan's money (that's what Oonagh called the compensation) into the business. I'll put more in when the house is sold."

"But we've been doing fine up 'til now." Marie had never seen Oonagh so on top of things.

"Yes but it's time to expand, time to look to the future, time for us to benefit for a change… agreed?"

Oonagh held out her hand. The two women's manly handshake cemented the deal and over the second pot of tea they drew up a list of things to do. By the end of the week Oonagh had three bank accounts and a decorator in her home. The house had been her future and Declan would have wanted her to get the best price for it. At tea with her mother and father that Sunday Oonagh told of her plans.

"Are you sure Oonagh that you want to move?" her mother, frightened of losing her, thought Derryvolgie Avenue a foreign territory.

"Yes Ma, I think it's right. Declan would have wanted me to keep on living – I just can't move on in that house without the boys."

Mother and daughter cried for their loss and silently folding an old linen tea towel the man of the house mourned with them. Over a comforting slice of buttered ginger cake and a cup of tea Oonagh offered her parents some money. They'd been so good to her for so long that any amount was not enough but they still thought the offer of £5000 excessive. Oonagh insisted and, with reluctance, they agreed to accept her gift. They wouldn't let her pay for the decorator. Proud people, they'd furnished their nest themselves and saw no reason why they shouldn't continue to do so.

"Ok, ok," conceded Oonagh. "I'll buy the paper and paint and you can pay for Ciaran."

Within two weeks a 'For Sale' sign decked Oonagh's family home and there was a second coat of emulsion on her parents' lounge. When Oonagh decided to do something there was no stopping her. How different from the schoolgirl she once was. Life had at last given her a sense of purpose. Marie's concerns and Oonagh's optimism balanced perfectly and the girls focussed on their Christmas bookings. Troy was helping them with a new act 'The Dream Boats' – four male strippers dressed as naval officers. So popular were they that Marie and Oonagh had offered Troy a percentage and a cash incentive to develop another group – 'The Outriders': four blokes dressed as motorcycle cops. By early December Troy had stopped stripping and under the banner of Downey Enterprises managed two male dancing troops. No longer could Marie run the business and keep her Strathearn residency and although she enjoyed singing she and Oonagh had big plans for Downey Enterprises and that is where the focus needed to be.

"Och," said the disappointed Scottish owner. "Won't you just do one last gig, New Year's Eve? I've already done the flyers." Marie looked at Oonagh – "Of course she'll do it Terence… you've been great for Marie and Downey Enterprises, how could we let you down?"

157

"But Oonagh…" protested Marie. "I thought we'd agreed…"

"Well, once last gig won't kill you and besides we'll be off on that cruise of a lifetime on the 5th so it will put you in fine form to challenge the competition."

Marie laughed. The cruise was supposed to be a holiday, but even she had to agree that if they managed to get a deal with a shipping line they'd be set up for life. Rory and the rest of the band took the news of Marie's retirement hard. Still, perhaps it was time for a change. Carmel and Rory had been going through a bad patch again. The pub was losing business and needed his full commitment, a commitment that Rory felt disinclined to give. Music was his first love, Carmel his second. They'd been together for so long that each had an individual agenda. Perhaps a new start in a new year wasn't a bad thing. Every two weeks Marie called the solicitors' to check up on the divorce papers. Every two weeks the answer was the same – they still couldn't trace Michael. Every two weeks Oonagh visited the Estate Agents to see if there was any movement on the house. Every two weeks the answer was the same – the property market was a little slow.

On 10th December everything changed. Oonagh took the call – a cash buyer was interested in her house and wanted a quick sale. He was moving up from Dublin with his wife and child and wanted to be in for Christmas. Would she accept £5000 under the asking price? Marie told Oonagh to hold on. The Bank Manager told her to hold on. Her parents told her to hold on. By 12th December she'd sold the family home.

Chapter Twenty

Brid Armstrong had had enough. The two boys were getting out of hand. She needed financial and psychological help. Now more than ever they needed a father and at last she had an address. All summer she scrimped and saved to afford the crossing. She thought of writing in advance but fearful that Michael would only scarper had decided on a surprise visit. She'd even lied to her sons. They were going to spend Christmas with an old cousin of hers. Brid was not only lying to the boys, she was lying to herself. Niall knew the real reason for the trip.

He was excited at the prospect of seeing his father – he wanted to kill him. That bastard had ruined his mother's life and needed to be taught a few lessons. Now nearly sixteen Niall had turned out all right. Sure he smoked some weed and drank too many beers but what boy of his age didn't? Sure his Ma wanted him to stay on at school, but what was the point? No one from his school ever got a decent job. Only dealers made a decent living. Still for the sake of his mother and his brother Sean he'd agreed to go to Ireland and meet this cousin he'd never heard of. Sean was also keen to get out of Christmas in Kilburn. Perhaps his Ma's cousin would be a laugh. Anything would be better than the last four years of Christmas apologies. The train journey to Liverpool was long. They each had a holdall to lug along the platform and Brid had an extra bag of sandwiches and biscuits for the journey. Niall ran ahead to find them seats together – a four with a table. They were lucky. Unlike Sean Niall could run fast and wasn't shy about standing his ground. He climbed onto a seat and lifted their bags above them. Brid arranged the contents of the carrier bag on the table and gave Niall money for buffet car teas. It took him ages and Sean and Brid were parched by the time he returned. Brid rationed the sandwiches – they'd have to last the journey for, on their budget, there was no room for fancy catering. Lunch finished, the boys donned their Walkmans and left their mother to her Maeve Binchy. There was little peace in the carriage for it was filled with festive Irish hope. Men forced into working exile-swilled cans of Guinness, single women with Civil Service jobs kept their eyes lowered, lads of one and twenty with road-induced acne longed for the farm. Goodwill warmth soon heated the carriage and as layers of wool were removed conversation was encouraged. The blue and grey fibrous seats provided little comfort. The longer the journey the harder they felt. An elderly nun got on at Crewe and sat beside Brid. Sister Francois smiled, this was her season and Brid returned the compliment. The twins kept their eyes lowered lest their sins be found out. Then the toilet run began. Sean was the first to bounce along the carriage and wait for the light to go out. Unlike Niall he couldn't and unlike Niall he didn't complain about the smell. Brid was next to go. She waited in the corridor as a large woman from Birmingham deposited a heavy lunch.

"You'd better be careful in there – what a mess." Brid folded some tissue on the seat and dared not look down. Who had been responsible for such a pebble dashing? Honestly – you couldn't take some people anywhere. After three attempts she raised a flush and with a foot-pump action managed to wash her hands. The only paper towels were on the floor and so she waved her hands in the air before gently brushing them against her skirt. Sister Francois was next to go.

God, thought Brid. *I hope she doesn't think I made that mess.*

On her return, the nun smiled sympathetically and Brid knew that the shit had been judged hers.

Niall carried Sister Francois' battered case up the gangplank and onto the boat. His mother had had a word and as it was the start of the holiday he thought it best to humour her.

"Thank you, son," said Sister Francois waddling off to find her cabin.

Brid Armstrong herded her sons together and joined the queue for cabin allocation. The ship smelled of oil and warm grilled cheese. The queue moved slowly and with heavy arms the Armstrongs eventually found their way to B deck and cabin 341. It was late. While Brid Armstrong found a toilet the boys dressed for bed. They were of an age – half boy, half man – that their bedroom was no place for her. She'd have preferred two cabins but a week in Belfast was expensive. Although her Lenadoon Avenue cousin was putting them up Brid didn't want to be a total burden. When she returned in her nightdress with her grey wool coat over the top the boys were still arguing over the bunks.

"Well, I'll take the bottom bunk," said Brid, "and that'll settle it once and for all."

It did and all three rolled with the tide towards Belfast.

December was madness for Oonagh and Marie. The agency was flat out keeping Northern Ireland audiences entertained. Marie was delighted to have Oonagh in the house full time especially as she had become a tough negotiator and had increased the fees all round.

Still, thought Marie, *only three more days and then a bloody day off at last.*

That year Christmas for all was to be in Derryvolgie Avenue. The girls had spent the last three Sundays decorating, organising sleeping arrangements and making lists of Christmas 'bits'. Sure, it was a break from tradition but it was time to change. This would be Oonagh's first Christmas in her new home and Marie wanted it to be perfect. They were all coming over on Christmas Eve; they'd have supper, go to Midnight Mass and do it all properly. On the wall chart in the office Oonagh had marked the days off in bright red and green and so on the morning of the 24th she and Marie started the final preparations for a great Christmas. Moira Downey was bringing the turkey from Larry's – already boned and stuffed for convenience. The ham from Sawers had been soaking for 24 hours and would be set to boil at 4pm prior to tomorrows roasting. Still in their dressing gowns the girls began to roll bacon onto bread sticks, defrock sprouts, peel potatoes, carrots and parsnips and make the special Downey stuffing. The Ormo Christmas cake and pudding had been purchased and while Oonagh went through their checklist Marie soaked in a Radox bath and thought of Christmases past.

Michael was still elusive. If only she could find him. If only the divorce would go through. Her lawyer had contacted the Sligo bitch and now she too was pursuing a broken relationship. Perhaps the New Year would sort it out. Her accountant was doing his best to sort the back tax. It would take a while but with Oonagh's investment and the Christmas figures Marie was certain that it would all work out fine.

As Oonagh made the Christmas trifle she talked with the boys. They'd loved to watch her dip the sponge fingers in sherry for lining the bowl. She hoped they were still watching her.

"Now, lads, I hope I've done the right thing in selling the house and moving in with Marie. I know she needs me but I really need you both to approve. It was very lonely in that house all on my own and Marie has been a good friend to all of us."

As she melted the red cubes of Chivers jelly and mixed in the Huntley's fruit cocktail Oonagh waited for an answer. None came.

"Now, come on boys, tell me it will be all right."

A customary sharp ring on the doorbell heralded Moira Downey.

"Don't look so worried, we're here now, it'll be alright. James, hurry up and carry that turkey in will you? It's far too heavy for me. Right Oonagh, here are some sausage rolls and mushroom patties from Bells. Oh, and I've made some of our special Downey stuffing!"

Oonagh smiled. How strange that the lads had used Moira Downey to communicate reassurance, she'd never have been capable of that on her own.

When Marie descended from her muscle relaxation the kitchen was in turmoil.

"Hi Dad! Great to see you – hello Mum."

Mr Downey smiled a greeting. His wife made a fuss.

"I've run your bath Oonagh. So why don't you have some quality time to yourself? Oh, and I've poured you out a glass of bubbly – it is Christmas Eve after all."

Oonagh left Moira, James and Marie and climbed the stairs to the bathroom. As she stepped into the warm soapy water she heard the behaviour of their childhood. Moira Downey was bossing her husband, advising her daughter, criticising the menu – it would be a great Christmas after all.

Chapter Twenty-One

Maeve O'Callaghan and her husband were running late. It was typical of Maeve – she could never visit Derryvolgie Avenue without twice checking that everything was just right. Now that Oonagh had moved in you'd have thought it might have been different – but you'd have thought wrong. Padraig O'Callaghan – patient as ever in the kitchen watched as his wife retied fine ribbons round the handmade gifts. She'd spent weeks handcrafting the Christmas boxes and now she needed more time for those all-important final touches.

"Padraig, where are the car keys?"

"Oh, here. I'll put them in the boot for you."

Instantly Padraig knew this was the wrong thing to say.

"They're not going in the boot – they'll get covered in dirt."

The boot being as clean as anything, he hoovered it out every Saturday, Padraig knew that this was impossible but he still nodded to his wife in agreement.

"Spread the car rug out on the back seat and I'll lay them out there."

One by one Maeve O'Callaghan carried the finely wrapped gifts to the car. She placed a bottle of sherry and a bottle of whiskey on the floor behind the passenger seat and watched as Padraig put their cases in the boot.

"Right, now off we go," encouraged Padraig, buttoning a driving glove, a Christmas present from Oonagh the previous year.

"I hope it'll be all right."

"It'll be grand Maeve, now stop worrying."

The two lonely grandparents set off on the fifteen-minute drive to Derryvolgie Avenue – their hearts pounding with what could have been their minds locked on what was.

"Och Ma and Da, how great to see you."

"Mr and Mrs O'Callaghan, come in, come in."

Reassured by the welcome the O'Callaghans entered a hall smelling of cinnamon and mince pies.

"What a beautiful tree – Padraig would you look at the tree?"

How typical that my mother notices nothing and that Oonagh finds pleasure in every detail. What a lovely way to be, thought Marie.

"Yes, Oonagh and I did it last Sunday."

"And the ribbons. Look at the lovely bows and the cut-glass balls – sure they're gorgeous."

"We've got some presents in the car. Shall I put them…?"

"There's another tree in the lounge… I think you'll like that too Mrs O'Callaghan."

All four of them gingerly carried the presents from the back seat of the car and placed them under the second Christmas tree.

"Now, that's just lovely," said Maeve stunned by the obvious expense.

"And look how your presents tie in – green and red with a little hint of gold – just like the tree itself."

Maeve O'Callaghan was delighted. Oonagh knew she would be for it was she who had suggested the colour scheme to Marie. Marie was equally thrilled by its success.

The men, James and Padraig, were sent down the Lisburn Road to get some logs for the Christmas Day fire. Marie gave them detailed instructions that took in O'Rourke's pub – sure a couple of whiskies couldn't do any harm. Besides, it would get her father out from under Moira Downey's critical eye. Oonagh buttoned up her Dad's overcoat and slipped a £20 note into his pocket – "Get a round in Dad and enjoy yourself." Padraig was too embarrassed to protest and the two men set off on foot for their three-hour adventure.

While Moira Downey filled mince pie cases and Marie hung that day's cards in the hall, Oonagh and her mother set about making the table centre. The girls had agreed that Maeve O'Callaghan would do a better job than any of them and had purchased wire, ribbon, oasis, candles, holly and some dark red roses to challenge her. To say that Oonagh helped is to lie. She watched in awe as her mother twisted wire round flower stems, tied perfect bows and placed spiralled gold candles in a line. Mrs O'Callaghan had forward planned. From her large handbag she produced tissue wrapped delights – single holly leaves wired and covered in gold glitter, berried ivy that had been given the same treatment and gilded polystyrene stars. An hour of toil created a masterpiece.

"My, that's spectacular," said Marie placing some homemade petit fours on the sideboard in the dining room.

"I think we all deserve a glass of sherry."

Maeve, who never drank, accepted a thimbleful of Bristol Cream and all four ladies toasted Christmas and the radiant centrepiece. The log bearing males were rewarded with a fourth whisky and the household was soon merry with dinner preparation.

Brid Armstrong's Lenadoon Avenue re-union had gone well. The boys had behaved themselves, that was something, and her cousin had said she hadn't changed a bit. It was a lie, but a kind one. That kindness encouraged Brid to explain the full reason for her being in Belfast and although her cousin Fidelma didn't fully understand why that bastard had to be traced, she promised to offer what support she could.

When the doorbell rang in Derryvolgie Avenue, the bacon sticks and mince pies were doing the rounds. Oonagh opened the door expecting carol singers but was greeted by no musical refrain –

"Hello, this may seem a bit odd but I'm looking for their father…"

The woman gestured to some fine looking boys

"And this is the last address we have…"

"Eh, you'd better come in," said Oonagh, showing them into the front room. Oonagh put the kettle on, grabbed Marie and a plate of mince pies and listened to the familiar ticking of the bomb. Calmly Brid introduced the party and, with the warmth of an old friend, told Oonagh and Marie her story. All the while Marie stared at Niall. He had a look about him, a look that she too easily recognised – that charm that had so impressed her about Michael Truesdale. When Brid had finished she produced a wrinkled christening photograph. The man struggling to hold the two boys was her husband.

"Well, he isn't here; he hasn't been for some time. I think you'd best stay and have something to eat."

"But I…" hesitated Brid.

"Trust me," interrupted Marie placing a hand on Brid's arm. "You'll need to."

While Marie announced the uninvited guests to the parents, Oonagh set three more places, gave the women sherry and the two boys a beer each and tried to gauge what was going on in Marie's head.

The boys had never seen such luxury. Frightened of damaging the plates they allowed their mother to serve them. Niall noticed her shaking hand; he'd never seen her so flustered. Marie began at what she thought was the beginning. The story, which should have started with her and Michael, now had a beginning that she knew nothing about. Still, she outlined the past with accuracy for it was the only way she knew. Brid felt for her – she'd been lied to. She'd been cheated on and she too had been abandoned. The quest to find the boys' father had merely turned up more wives. They could all have done without this.

As she rinsed down the remnants of leek and potato soup even Moira Downey was silent. She was dying to ask what all this meant for Marie and the divorce but James' firm hand on her arm compelled her to keep her questions to herself. Oonagh passed round the heated plates and willed these people to leave. She needed to comfort her friend. They'd spent so many years sorting out his mess and just as they were getting on track – bang.

"He's just a two-timing shite mum. We should forget about him."

"Now, Niall. He wasn't always like that."

"Well," said Marie. "That's what I thought too, but we are only two women in his life of how many? It's time that bastard paid for what he has done."

"I only wanted the boys to meet their father. I didn't want to cause any harm."

"Look, the harm was done long ago and not by you. I'll track that bastard down if it kills me. It's what he deserves. You can decide to meet him or not. It's up to you. Unlike you I've nothing more to lose – roast potatoes lads?"

Oonagh stopped worrying. Marie had taken control of the situation; there could be no more revelations to shock her now. Her marriage was worthless, perhaps illegal and there'd be little need for that divorce. By vowing to help Brid Marie had convinced herself of the need to finally confront Michael Truesdale. She needed to cry at his grave before she could move on.

After several attempts Marie got a taxi to take her… well what exactly were they? Were they nephews or were they no relation? They were guests that would just have to do… back to Lenadoon Avenue. She'd invited them over on Boxing Night. Christmas Day was all about family after all.

"Well, what are we to make of all that?" enquired Moira Downey unable to keep her silence as they cleared the dining table.

"They are good looking boys," said Oonagh.

"Yes, but is that Michael Truesdale one, your husband, the father?"

"He's not my husband, mother and if there was any doubt he's the father of those boys you only have to look at the Niall one. It's all in the eyes. He's Michael's son."

"But what does she want Marie, what does she want?"

"Oonagh, what do you think?"

"I suspect she just wants the boys to know who their father is."

"Well, after tonight, they know what he is that's for sure."

"Now Marie," said James Downey. "I think we've all had enough for one night. It's the season of goodwill after all."

The men prepared the fires for the morning. The mothers re-arranged the presents under the tree and with two large vodka and tonics Marie and Oonagh wondered, "What the fuck next?"

As they peeled root vegetables and sipped their second V&T the girls talked over the evening. Tomorrow was Christmas Day and they'd be damned if any ghost of Michael Truesdale's past would be able to destroy that.

"I can understand him not wanting children with me, he already had two boys of his own but why did he have them with that Sligo bitch?"

Oonagh, noting the long suppressed anger in her friend, had no answers.

"Perhaps he got caught out; perhaps the child isn't his after all."

"It's her I feel sorry for…"

"What? Your woman in Sligo?"

"No, Brid, she's obviously had a hard life and here she is trying to do the right thing… and look where it has got her."

"You know Marie Downey… sometimes you surprise me."

"You know Oonagh, sometimes I surprise myself."

"So what will you do now?"

"More potatoes I think… you know how hungry those Das of ours get after a few jars."

Oonagh knew when to keep quiet. She handed Marie another bag of Whites.

Chapter Twenty-Two

Christmas Day was spent in wonderment. In Lenadoon Avenue, while sprouts were crossed and the small turkey basted, Brid Armstrong thought of the woman he had abandoned. She seemed to have everything – great friends, a caring family and money, loads of money, and yet he had walked out on her too. Then there was the third woman, the one in Sligo. She hoped that neither son had inherited their father's love-loathing of women. Now, not only had she the father to find, but also there was a stepbrother maybe a stepsister to look out for. All her life Brid Armstrong had looked out for her boys. Had she made a mistake bringing them to Ireland? What had she been thinking? Michael had stayed away after all and if he hadn't wanted to be traced why had he sent out of date clues for birthdays and at Christmas? Fidelma poured out two glasses of Liebfraumilch.

"Here," she said, handing some fake crystal to Brid. "Get that down you. Happy Christmas!"

"Happy Christmas," said one and all in Derryvolgie Avenue. Oonagh and Marie had done themselves proud. Not even the Christmas Eve arrivals had put the girls off their stride. It was only over coffee and petit fours that the subject was raised.

"So Marie, what are you going to do now?"

It was odd that her father should bring it up. Obviously, the Downey parents had been up all night discussing it and for once had developed a unified strategy.

"Well, as I told that woman Brid yesterday, I'll find him. Those boys need to see just what kind of man their father is and I need to know just whose husband he really is. Look on the bright side, at least now I'll save on the divorce."

"We'll have to let the police know, Marie," said Oonagh.

"Oh don't worry; I'll have a word with Inspector O'Flaherty tomorrow night. Dad, will that bloody solicitor turn up for a change?"

"Don't worry Marie; I've made sure of that."

"Well then, let's enjoy the Two Ronnies and say no more about it."

Moira Downey sucked at the homemade truffles in a desperate attempt to do as her daughter had asked. Her slurping grew so loud that both Marie and Oonagh would have preferred her to just spit it out. It was always so obvious when Moira Downey had something to say but with James squinting at her from across the lounge she knew she couldn't break her promise.

No one really wanted to watch Oliver or Kind Hearts and Coronets but it gave them something to do before supper. Over cold cuts and chutney the room relaxed.

"They are two good looking boys," said James Downey.

"And well mannered, for Englishmen," said Oonagh.

"They have their mother to thank for that no doubt," said Moira Downey.

"Do you know Mum, I think you are right."

The room fell silent for this was a turning point. It was the first time in years that mother and daughter had agreed on anything. Maeve O'Callaghan smiled at her daughter. The two fathers nodded at each other. All realised that an entente cordiale had occurred.

Chapter Twenty-Three

Apart from those at the hunt, Ireland rose late on Boxing Day. Bloated from the previous Day's excesses, Marie and Oonagh sipped cold coffee as they set about organising the furniture for the evening event. All morning the girls, for that's what they were when they were together, talked of the pending holiday. As the men vacuumed and the wives defrosted jus-rol vol-au-vent cases, Oonagh and Marie made saucy fillings – creamy mushroom, white fish cheese sauce, chicken and parsley sauce and soon the four women in the house began their party production line. Vol-au-vents complete, the same line attacked roast chickens, uncooked rice, raw fruit and vegetables and soon bowls of coronation chicken, savoury rice and fruit salad were ready to be cling-filmed. The garage freezer offered up cheesecakes and profiteroles and by 6.30 that evening the Boxing Day Buffet was complete. James Downey had enlisted Padraig's help in the creation of alcoholic and non-alcoholic punch. The only difference in the mixture was the alcohol and boy did that make a difference. Troy was first to arrive with his Civil Service boyfriend and both his dancing troupes. Even off duty the boys looked oily and Moira Downey feared for her daughter's leather suite. By eight o'clock the house was full of old and new friends. Brid and her sons need not have worried, everyone was very friendly and Niall seemed quite at home with the 'Outriders'. Rory set up the band in the corner of the living room and soon the party was in full swing.

Marie was only half way through 'Crazy', her second request of the night, when Inspector O'Flaherty arrived. He was with two uniformed officers and not his wife.

"Sorry Marie, could we have a word?"

Marie walked through to the kitchen with Oonagh following behind her.

"Ladies, I think we have found your husband."

"Great, where is the bastard?" shrieked Marie, all those years of concealed anger bursting forth.

"I need you to make a formal identification of course but we have reason to believe he died in a house fire…"

The words all merged into a haze. Oonagh heard her old address. Marie heard of a mother and child, arriving at the kitchen door Moira and James Downey heard insurance scam and Eamonn and Maeve O'Callaghan heard only crying.

Brid Armstrong heard none of this. She was singing Danny Boy for all she was worth.

Michael Truesdale's death, like his life, was suspicious. The corpse belonged to him and Michael Armstrong and Michael Dale and to God knows how many other Michaels at home and abroad. Marie had felt little when the cold sheet was lifted. It was him all right. How she'd feared identifying his drowned body all those years ago but it was fire, not water that had put an end to Michael Truesdale. Marie had often wished him in hell but she'd never have thought it meant this. Oonagh too was in a state of shock. What had he been doing in her old house? Some sort of property investor, the police said. He bought places, did them up and sold them on at a vast profit. Well, that's what Michael Hennessey did. The wallet in the charred jacket had lead the police to Derryvolgie Avenue for it still contained Michael Truesdale's driving licence. It is strange how a body can enliven a police investigation and Marie and Oonagh spent the next two days helping with enquiries. Brid too was questioned, much to the annoyance of cousin Fidelma, who had never met a member of the RUC. Marie called Theresa Coyne and the RUC alerted the Garda. After some debate Marie and Oonagh decided to do the decent thing and have him buried from the house. No one else had a better plan even though they had spent days discussing it. Cause of death? "Asphyxiation due to smoke inhalation." Michael Truesdale had been doing some re-wiring and after a heavy day had fallen asleep with a bottle of scotch. He tried to get down the stairs but had collapsed. No one had come to his aid. No one knew he was there. In death, as in life, Michael Truesdale had tried to be secretive. But secrets come out, no matter how well they are buried, and not even Michael Truesdale could prevent this truth from appearing.

For days the house was full of people. Rory, Carmel and Troy made endless cups of tea, James Downey diluted whisky and Oonagh and the two mothers made so many ham sandwiches that they wished they were Jewish. Death notices were placed in the Sligo Herald and the Belfast and Dublin papers. Although they'd put 'house private', Marie was sure lots of people would turn up. She herself became a news item as the coffin arrived in the driveway. All day the telephones rang.

"They are only doing their job Oonagh."

"Well, you'd think they'd show a little respect."

Marie laughed.

"Do you think that's what he deserves after all this?"

"It's you I'm thinking of…"

James Downey sought advice, advice from the police, the family solicitor, advice from everyone but his wife and in the end it was agreed that Marie should issue a statement.

"Bollocks to that." It was agreed by all except Marie.

"We are finally going to make some money out of this mess – what do you say, Brid?"

For the first time in his life, Michael Truesdale was exclusive. One TV channel, one radio station and one newspaper were selected and Brid and Marie told their story. James Downey, Troy and Oonagh sat in as impartial witnesses. They monitored the incredulity of the journalists.

"I hope you have done the right thing," said Oonagh as the press people left.

"Well, I feel better for it. We've lived under his shadow for too long. Besides, it'll mean more spending money for the cruise."

Chapter Twenty-Four

Two days later, Michael Truesdale was interred. Marie wore a black Jaeger coat with a black and white Escada dress. Oonagh had put a new colour in Marie's hair and she looked great. Brid had found a coat in the sales and Marie had lent her a black cloche that she never wore. Perhaps it was best that the boys never met their father. What lies he could have told. What a charmer he could have been. It rained from early on that morning. The undertakers were punctual and efficient. The drawing room was full of women and children, all with a family connection.

Theresa Coyne and her husband had driven up the night before and had stayed with friends in Comber.

"So," wondered Theresa, "where's that red head and her wee bastard?"

The Sligo girl that had unleashed another double identity was at home crying for her lost love and wondering how to support the children. Even if he had left a lot of money she was certain there would be many in line before her. What use the upheaval? What use attending a funeral in Belfast? She had to think of herself and the kids now.

Brid, Niall and Sean huddled near the sideboard. They were like strangers in a familiar place. Niall's father had been dead to him for many years. He'd only come to keep the peace at home. Sean, although upset, couldn't reconcile the man his mother talked about with the bloke in the box next door. Their mother eyed the brassy Dublin blonde who sniffled on a velvet armchair. It was obvious why he had gone for her, all too obvious.

In the kitchen Moira Downey was ashamed. Now everyone knew her daughter's business. How would she ever be able to walk down Holywood High Street again? Oonagh stood by her friend.

At last, she thought. *There's an end to all this wondering. Marie can finally move on.*

Troy put a comforting arm around Marie and they all filed out to the cars. Oonagh and Marie kept their heads lowered as photographers tried to identify the other wives. Marie thought that the drive up to Redburn Cemetery would put them off. She was right. The driveway and a couple of well-fed police officers were deterrent enough.

The vicar who had married them, or not married them, said a few words and the undertakers lowered Michael Truesdale into the ground and between the mounds of earth and the grave's edge stood the high-heeled women of his past.

They each have a story to tell, thought Oonagh, *but who knows which of their stories is true?*

Oonagh held Marie's hand as she sobbed into a crumpled lace handkerchief.

"You know Oonagh I loved him, I loved him."

"I know Marie, I know."

Moira Downey moved as if to comfort her daughter but sliding mud prevented her. Black patent shoes acquired from Reids for Christmas were not made for grieving. James Downey put a hand on his daughter's shoulder –

"You'll be all right love, you'll be all right," he murmured.

Oonagh's parents watched her from across the graveside. They were so proud of her. She was a survivor and day-by-day was giving Marie the support that once she'd had. That was as it should be.

In the rain Oonagh and Marie looked at the sodden cards that adorned the flowers. Old acts, long since retired, sent memories of happier days. Yet most of the flowers that were signed with love came from women. Just how many had had their sex weakened by Michael Truesdale?

"You'll come back to the house with the boys, Brid?"

"You know Marie, I don't think we will. You've been great but I need to be on my own with the family – you understand?"

"Of course, but you will stay in touch? We might have a few job offers for those boys of yours."

"We will. I'll give you a call. I think we'll be in Belfast for a while. Look after yourself."

A leggy blonde walked down the hill towards the Cemetery gates.

"Pull over!" said Marie to the driver.

"Can we give you a lift?"

"Well, I need to get to the Park Avenue Hotel…"

"Hop in," said Oonagh.

"Are you sure you don't mind?"

"Not at all," laughed Marie. "Sure any friend of Michael's is a friend of ours."

Oonagh chuckled and soon all three were in fits of laughter. Tears ran down their cheeks.

"God, he was some boy that one," said the latest Truesdale conquest.

"He sure was," smiled Marie. "He sure was."

Oonagh looked back in agreement.